THE ODDS OF LOVING GROVER CLEVELAND

ALSO BY REBEKAH CRANE

Aspen

Playing Nice

THE ODDS OF LOVING GROVER CLEVELAND

a novel

REBEKAH CRANE

This is a work of fiction. Names, characters, organizations, places, events, and incidents are either products of the author's imagination or are used fictitiously.

Published by Skyscape, New York

www.apub.com

ISBN-13: 9781503939820
ISBN-10: 1503939820

Cover design by Adil Dara

Printed in the United States of America

For Kyle—who knows all about my crazy and loves me for it.

Dear Future Campers—

Camp Padua welcomes you to a summer of exploration, adventure, and above all self-discovery. We work toward the highest level of personal growth and healing. In order to best serve you, our campers, our highly trained counselors focus on six essential qualities all people must possess. Without them, we are lost.

We ask that over the next five weeks, you think about the person you are . . . and the person you need to become.

—The Staff

KNOWING YOURSELF

CHAPTER 1

Mom and Dad,

They told me I had to write this. Camp is fine. I'll see you soon.

Z

PS—I'm fine, too . . . no matter what you think.

The doorknob locks with a single key from the inside of the cabin. My bag hangs over my shoulder as I stare at the silver knob like it might start talking. This can't be legal.

"We only lock the doors at night for precautionary reasons. And I sleep in the cabin with you," Madison says, tugging on the key dangling from her neck. She touches my arm. I glance down at her finely painted fingernails pressing into my skin. The magenta polish has a glossy layer of perfection.

"What is there to be cautious about?" I ask.

Madison doesn't answer me right away. She gives me one of those half smiles and cocks her head to the side, like she's thinking about what to say next. She picks up her long brown braided hair and inspects the end of it.

"It keeps the bears out." She pulls a split end free.

"I didn't think there were bears here."

"The woods around here are filled with a lot of things people don't want to admit exist. But don't worry. That's what I'm here for." She touches my arm again.

Madison is dressed in a hunter-green T-shirt with the camp's logo across the front and black cargo shorts. Her bright nail polish contrasts with her outdoorsy outfit. It doesn't match.

"I remember my first time at camp. I was *so* nervous," Madison says.

"Did you go here?"

"No . . ." Madison trails off. She fiddles with her shirt, smoothing down the front of it. "It was a horse camp in California."

Madison looks like a girl who grew up wealthy enough to ride horses and wear pink polo shirts and white shorts with whales on them. It would match her nail polish perfectly.

"I'm not nervous," I say.

"That's good." Madison smiles. "Well, get yourself situated and we'll meet in the Circle of Hope in a half hour."

"The Circle of Hope. Why there?" I ask.

"If we don't have hope, Zander, we don't have anything. It's the best place to start." She touches my arm and smiles one more time before walking away, her braid swishing across her back.

"That's not an answer," I mumble as a mosquito buzzes in my face. I swat it away, but it's back within seconds. A door that locks and unlocks from the inside by a single key has to be a fire hazard. I'm right. This is totally illegal. Maybe I could report this place and get it shut down, but then I'd have to go home.

I drop my bag on the ground. It makes a dull thud on the cement floor. Other than the cold concrete beneath my feet, everything in the room is wood—the beds, the walls, the dressers. I sit down on the bare mattress of one of the beds and run my hands through my hair, pulling a little too hard. A few black strands pop loose. I can't seem to break the habit though it makes my thin hair even thinner and more lightweight.

"Crap," I murmur to myself.

The door flies open, smacking against the wood wall with a bang.

A girl dressed in the smallest white tank top and shortest red shorts I've ever seen stands in the doorway.

"Talking to yourself isn't a good sign," she says, circling her index finger next to her temple.

She flings her bag onto the bed. I stare at her. I can't help it. She's not wearing a bra. What girl doesn't wear a bra under a thin white tank top? Her dark brown skin shows through the shirt. *All* her skin. Even her nipples.

"What?" she barks at me.

She's skinny, too, like the kind of skinny that gets you hospitalized. *Gaunt* might be a better term. She is practically hollow.

She plops down on the bed, crossing her long legs.

"I'm Cassie," she states but doesn't hold out her hand. "I know. It's a fat girl's name." Before I can get my name out, Cassie proceeds to dump the contents of her duffel bag out on the bed. I scan the pile of clothes looking for a bra of any kind, but all I see is a hot-pink bikini, short shorts, and tank tops in multiple colors. Cassie takes an armful of clothes and says, "I take it you met Madison." She stuffs them into a drawer without folding or separating the items. She just shoves all the chaos into one space. "She's a fucking moron."

As she talks, Cassie grabs her empty bag and turns it upside down. A waterfall of pill containers splatters onto the bed.

"Like I said, these counselors are idiots. They don't even check the pockets." She pops the top on a bottle. "Don't stare. It's rude," she says.

"Sorry." I look down at my hands.

"I'm kidding. Everyone stares, especially here." Cassie holds out a handful of pills to me, an offering. "Diet pills. You want some?"

I shake my head. "I hate pills."

"Suit yourself, but I'd stay away from the macaroni in the mess hall." Cassie puffs out her cheeks and points at me. I can't help but look down at my body. No one would ever call me skinny, but I'm not fat. My mom would never allow that.

I tug at my yellow T-shirt so it's not so tight. "Noted."

She tosses the pills into her mouth and swallows them without water. "So why are you here?" she asks.

"What?"

"Is it because you're deaf?" Cassie makes a fake frown face and enunciates every word, speaking louder. *"Why are you here?"*

"I'm not deaf."

"No shit, moron. That's a different kind of camp."

I play with the front of my T-shirt, picking a mosquito off it. Why *am* I here? Looking at the girl in front of me, we're nowhere near the same. I don't belong lumped in a group with her. I squish the mosquito hard between my fingers and say, "I'm here because my parents signed me up."

Cassie laughs so loud it echoes in the bare cabin. The noise rattles me. "So you're one of those."

"One of those?"

"A fucking moron and a liar."

I sit up straighter. Did a girl who eats diet pills for breakfast and refuses to wear a bra just call me a liar?

"Uh-oh, did I make you mad?" Cassie mocks.

"No," I say.

"Well, I can't help it. I'm a manic-depressive-bipolar-anorexic disaster. Self-diagnosed. And some days I think I'm a boy living in a girl's body." She stands up. "But at least I'm honest about who I am. Just remember, people who are *really* crazy don't know they're crazy."

She stuffs the pills back into the hidden pocket of her duffel bag and shoves the bag under the bed. Before she leaves, she glances down at my luggage to the name written on the outside. "Zander? That's your name?" She shakes her head. "Yep. Definitely crazy. Have fun talking to yourself, *Zander*."

Cassie disappears out the door. For a moment, I consider telling Madison about her pharmacy of pills hidden in her bag, but something tells me that getting on Cassie's bad side for the next five weeks isn't a good idea.

I take a breath of the heavy air and stare up at the wooden ceiling. One match would light this place on fire if it could get past the humidity. But burning down a cabin would send me home and prove that Cassie is right—that I am crazy.

And I can't be crazy. It would make my parents too happy. And as far as going home, I don't want to be in my house. Not with how it is now.

My parents didn't even ask if I wanted to come here. We sat down to dinner a few months ago and it was announced. I swirled my spaghetti around my fork as my parents talked about me like I wasn't even in the room. To be fair, I had a huge French test the next day, and I was conjugating verbs in the *passé composé* tense in my head.

J'ai mangé

Tu as mangé

Il a mangé

Nous avons mangé

Vous avez mangé

Ils ont mangé

"This is exactly why she needs to go," my mom complained, still talking about me like I wasn't in the room.

The conjugating is a habit now. My grade at the end of the year was practically an A+.

"When you get back, all of this will be a memory. You'll be a different person," my mom said the night before I left, as my boyfriend and I sat around a bowl of organic vegetables and dip. I've been dating Coop for two years. His real name is Cooper. I've never told him, but I think both options are pretty terrible. Coop sounds like a date-raping football player who crushes beers on his head. And calling him Cooper sounds like I'm hollering for a dog.

I snapped a carrot in my mouth and nodded at my mom. The crunching sound was so loud in my ears it blocked out what everyone was saying.

When I'd eaten the entire bowl, I pulled Coop up to my room and we made out. It was the high point of the evening. And Coop isn't that great of a kisser. He's kind of slobbery, like a dog named Cooper.

When I got bored, I conjugated verbs. Kissing and conjugating go well together. They're both French.

No. Going home isn't an option, so I pick a dresser to unload my clothes, separating them into shirts, pants, and underthings including the pile of bras my mom packed. She set my bag at the foot of my bed the day I left and said, "There. All done."

In French, *fini*.

She should have used those words years ago, but my mom isn't one for letting go of things.

I take the bottom bunk, thinking it will be easier to get out of this place if it lights on fire and if I can get past the locked door. When I pull the sheets and quilt my mom has packed for bedding from my bag, my whole body sags. The tiredness is back, like gravity just doubled and my knees want to give out, but I force myself to make the bed, sure to do hospital corners like my mom taught me.

When I'm done, I stare at my neat work. A mosquito buzzes in my ear and I smack my hands together trying to kill it, but I miss. It's back within seconds.

"Damn it." I shake my head clear. But my bed sits there staring back at me. It's as if there are a pair of eyes and a body and lungs just under the sheets, trying so hard to breathe. Trying hard but failing. Because, in the end, we all fail. We all sink to the bottom, no matter how many times someone tries to pull us back to the surface.

When I can't stand looking at my finely made bed any longer, I mess it all up. I tear out the hospital corners and stuff the thin pastel flower quilt back in my bag, not caring if it's folded properly, just that it's out of sight. I sit down on the bed, out of breath, my chest heaving hard.

I'd rather freeze every night than sleep with that stuff.

"Fini," I say. Shit. Talking to myself again. I look around, making sure no one saw me. But I'm alone. My family is across the country in Arizona and I'm in the middle of Michigan. I try hard to be sad about that fact, but it's as if I'm grabbing for something that isn't there. All I get is a handful of nothing. I'm just empty.

I walk out of the cabin into the swamp-like hot day, unsure of what to do next. But one thing is clear. I'd better stop talking to myself or people here will get the wrong idea.

CHAPTER 2

Dear Mom and President Cleveland,

The odds of finding love are one in 285,000, but the probability of getting married is 80 percent. There seems to be a discrepancy here.

Your son,

Grover Cleveland

My parents told me a few months ago where exactly I would spend the summer. My dad put up his hand and pointed to the center of it.

"It's right here, Zander. That's where the camp is located," he said. "Get it? Michigan is shaped like a glove."

I didn't respond so my mom added, "Arizona is miserable in the summer anyway. It's a million degrees. You'll like being away from here." She looked at my dad with thin, tight lips. "Even if it is undesirable that you should be carted halfway across the world without your parents."

"We agreed on this together, so don't start with the hyperbole, Nina. The camp isn't in India," my dad said.

I watched a fly struggle in a spiderweb as my parents fought at the dinner table. I understood the fly well. No matter which way it turned, it was caught. What's the use in fighting? You only end up more tangled.

"Camp Padua has seven distinct areas. The boys' quarters, the girls' quarters, the mess hall, the beach, the archery field, the stables, and most importantly—the Circle of Hope." Madison gave me a tour when I'd arrived. She directed me across campus pointing this way and that. "Lots of options. It should be a lot of fun this summer, too. Not all . . ." She paused and looked at me. "Business. What are you into?"

I didn't know what to say.

"You know, what's your *thing*?" Madison asked again with a smile.

I didn't respond and, after a while, Madison gave up on waiting for an answer. The truth is, I don't have a thing. Life is better that way.

"Girls must stay in the girls' quarters and boys in the boys'. The summer may not be all business, but we don't want any funny business either," Madison said, nudging my side.

"I have a boyfriend," I said.

Madison perked up. "You do? That's great. I remember my high school boyfriend. First love is so exciting."

"We don't love each other," I said. "He just likes my boobs."

We moved on from the subject.

She pointed out the mess hall and the paths that lead back to the stables. We finally got to the archery field and the Circle of Hope, which, it turns out, would be called a fire pit at any other place. Then she took me down to the lake.

"This is Lake Kimball. We ask that all campers refrain from going into the lake until the swim test is administered. We don't want any accidents." Madison looked at me. "And wear sunscreen. You're like me. It only takes about five minutes in the sun to cook us through."

I nodded. My mom likes to think I take after her Native American side with my black hair and almond eyes, but my skin would prove otherwise. Madison is right. I turn bright red if exposed to the sun for too long, a trait from my dad. But she's wrong about everything else. I am nothing like her.

Just the thought of cold water brings my body temperature down. The camp may not be in India, but you wouldn't know that by the humidity. Presently my hair is stuck to my neck, and I can feel sweat running down my back.

I take a detour on my walk to the Circle of Hope and head toward the lake. Trees speckle the entire grounds of Camp Padua. My dad pointed out how green everything is when he dropped me off. We drove through the gates of Camp Padua and he said, "Everything is just so alive here."

I nodded but didn't respond. I was too focused on the tall wire fence that lines the camp property. Green branches and bushes pushed out through the holes in the chain links.

When I asked why fencing surrounded the camp, he said, "To make sure everyone stays safe."

"Safe," I said quietly. My dad and I both know that no matter how hard you try, it's impossible to keep a person completely safe. Even when you ship them across the country to Michigan for the summer.

The staircase to the beach is just past the big wooden mess hall that separates the girls' side from the boys' side of camp. There's not a single ripple on the lake. I wipe a bead of sweat from my cheek.

Most campers are still attached to their parents, saying their good-byes. Once my dad checked me in at the admissions office, he bolted. "I have to get back to the airport if I'm going to make my flight," he said, and kissed me on the cheek. I didn't mind. A good-bye is a good-bye whether it's a long one or not.

Down at the lake, I take off my old, beat-up tennis shoes and socks and dip my feet in the water. The sand is squishy between my toes, like slime, but it's cold. A chill runs up my feet to my legs to my waist to the top of my head, and I stop sweating almost instantly.

I step in farther so the water comes up to my knees. I can't see my feet at the bottom; the water is too murky and full of lake weed. A person could get lost underneath it and just . . . disappear.

I close my eyes and imagine sinking through the layers of cold slime to the bottom. Like drowning in one of my mom's thick spinach smoothies. My knees bend closer to the water as I take another step. There's nothingness down at my feet—vast, empty space where a person could just let go. The pressure of feeling and then feeling nothing doesn't exist. Just darkness does. I know that place. I've been there before.

"Hey you!" A voice bellows from the top of the staircase. I whip around, startled. A male counselor with blond hair down to his shoulders stands like the warden at a jail with his hands on his hips. "Campers are not allowed to access the water on the first day."

"Sorry," I say as I pull my socks onto wet feet.

"Please make your way over to the Circle of Hope." He motions toward the fire pit before walking away.

Cassie is standing next to Madison when I arrive. She's pulling a large piece of pink bubble gum out of her mouth and twisting it around her finger. When she catches me staring, she wraps the gum around her middle finger and smiles. It's not a real smile. It's more like a warning covered in cotton-candy bubble gum.

"Over here, Zander," Madison bellows at me. "Zander, this is Katie, Hannah, and Dori. Cassie tells me you two have already met."

Cassie points her long skinny finger at a girl with mousy blonde hair and hazel eyes. "Katie, here, is the bingeing and purging type."

"Cassie," Madison barks.

"What?" Cassie snaps a hard look at Madison and grabs Katie's hand. "Do you see her throw-up fingers? The skin is practically bare from her stuffing them so far down her throat. I know an eating problem when I see one."

Katie shrugs and says, "She's right."

"See? I should be a counselor here." Cassie looks back at me. "Hannah is a cutter. See how she wears long sleeves in the fucking dead of summer? I bet she's got scars all up and down those chubby stems."

Hannah crosses her arms, which *are* covered in a navy-blue long-sleeved shirt. "I'm not chubby," she says but doesn't deny the cutting part.

"And Dori is depressed, which is totally boring. Every teenager is depressed. It's what we do best."

"I think that's enough." Madison puts her hand on Cassie's shoulder, but she shrugs it off.

Cassie turns her eye on me and says to the group, "And *Zander* is here because her 'parents signed her up.'" She cocks her head to the side and all four girls start laughing. "But I caught her talking to herself, so I'm not ruling out multiple personalities."

"I don't have multiple personalities," I say.

"Schizophrenia?" Hannah asks. Her dark brown eyes focus on me like I'm a lab rat.

"No." I glare at Cassie.

"That's enough, girls." Madison comes to stand behind me, placing both of her hands on my shoulders. I notice her pristine nail polish again. I don't need her coming to my aid. I don't need anybody. As far as I'm concerned, I just wish everyone and everything would disappear and leave me alone.

I shrug away Madison's hands and move to stand in a different part of the circle. I don't belong in that group. I don't like blood, let alone self-inflicted pain, and making yourself vomit? I hate when I puke and little bits of food get stuck in my nostrils. Why would someone do that on purpose?

I move between the sea of campers all huddled together, trying to find a spot where I can be alone and away from everyone. It may not be what my parents want for me this summer, for me to be isolated, but they have never asked me what I wanted. If they did, all of this could have been avoided. I wouldn't need to be here, swarmed by almost fifty kids with a load of counselors and staff circling the group. And no way out. I'm trapped.

When an older guy who's dressed in the same Camp Padua shirt as Madison stands up on a bench and claps three times, the circle goes still and silent. I freeze in place.

"The only way to be found," he yells.

"Is to admit we're lost," the rest of the counselors ring back in chorus.

"Welcome to Camp Padua," he continues through the silence. Brown hair hangs shaggy over his forehead, and he tucks it behind his ears before continuing. He looks older than Madison but younger than my parents, midthirties maybe, and handsome in a president-of-a-fraternity kind of way. "I'm Kerry, the owner of Camp Padua. I want to welcome everyone today." And when Kerry smiles, his looks improve even more. "I founded this camp over ten years ago in hopes of helping teens just like you find their way through the tough times. It's nice to see both familiar and new faces out there. If you need anything, don't hesitate to come and talk to me. This summer is about opening up, letting go, and finding your way back to who you truly are. Every counselor here has been through a rigorous training program to help you during your stay at camp. But above all, we want you to have a fun summer. And to have fun, you need to follow the rules for optimum safety."

A wave of exhaustion hits me as Kerry goes over the rules. Numbness creeps up my legs and spine and, for a moment, I think I could actually fall asleep standing up. It's the best I've felt all day, just sinking into a dazed stupor. When he gets to the rule about no food in the cabin, I almost raise my hand and ask if popping diet pills like candy counts as food, but that would mean raising my hand. Instead, I stare down at the ground, pushing dirt around with my shoe, and conjugate.

J'ai fini
Tu as fini
Il a fini

"Rule number four: If you are on any kind of medication, you must continue taking it at camp. The nurse will dispense all meds in the morning and evening at the Wellness Center. See her immediately if you have any shift in mood or think you might harm yourself."

Nous avons fini

Vous avez fini

"You'd think this camp is for crazy people the way this guy talks." I glance up at the boy next to me. He's about a million feet tall. I have to put my hand up to my eyes to block the sun just to look at him.

"I don't think it's for crazy people. I know it is," I whisper.

"'Kids with heightened mental or emotional states,' I believe is what the brochure says. Technically every teenager is in a heightened emotional state. At least boys are. I think about sex a hundred times a day, which definitely makes for a heightened emotional state. And a physical one for that matter." The boy looks down at his crotch.

"You think about sex that much?"

"Yes."

I glance back at Kerry. I don't know what to say to this boy. We're already talking about sex and I don't even know his name.

"And food," the boy whispers.

"What?"

"Food. Boys think about food a lot, too." He bends down closer to my ear. "Just in case you were wondering."

I nod, unsure of where this is going. "Do you want me to tell you what girls think about?"

"No. Then I'll have to think about it and I'm already busy thinking about food and sex. The mind can only take so much." He taps on his temple. "I don't want to push it. Heightened emotional state, remember."

"Right," I say and go back to staring at the ground. But every few seconds, I look up at him. He's skinny and long everywhere, like he'll probably fill out when he goes to college, but right now his metabolism is so high he can't eat enough to keep up. Brown hair hangs over his blue-brown eyes, which are too big for his face, like he's a cartoon character, but not a prince cartoon. The quirky sidekick, maybe.

"Rule number ten," Kerry says, practically yelling. "Boys sleep in the boys' quarters. Girls sleep in the girls' quarters."

The boy next to me raises his hand to ask a question. "What about the girls who think they might be boys? Where do they sleep?"

Kerry crosses his arms over his chest. "In the girls' quarters."

"Just checking." The boy nods at Kerry and smiles down at me again. My stomach gets tight. Tight like I just did twenty-five crunches in gym class. The feeling startles me.

"I'm Grover, by the way," the boy whispers. "Grover Cleveland."

CHAPTER 3

Cher Papa,

J'ai été enlevé par des étrangers. S'il te plaît, envoie de l'aide.

Cordialement,

Alex Trebek

Kerry tells us that every day we are allowed to pick between an array of activities ranging from arts and crafts to horseback riding, but the longer he talks, the harder it becomes to concentrate on anything but the boy next to me.

"You are in charge of your path," Kerry says. "The counselors are here to guide you, but you're old enough to make your own decisions. The only daily requirement is that you attend your cabin's group therapy session." He finishes his speech and tells us that dinner is in an hour. The sun shines in my eyes as I stare up at the kid next to me.

"Grover Cleveland? Like the president?" I say.

Grover nods and reaches into his back pocket. He pulls out a small notebook and pen. "And you are?"

I step back from him and run through the list of disorders Cassie rattled off. "Do you think you're Grover Cleveland or is that your real name?"

"Being real is key here. Are *you* real?"

"Yes, I'm real."

Grover taps his pen to his chin and shakes his head. "But if you were imaginary, you would still say you're real just to make me *think* you're real. So that line of questioning won't work."

"What?"

"I'm trying to determine if you're real."

"I just told you that I'm real."

"That doesn't prove anything. Stomp on my foot."

"What?" I ask.

"Stomp on my foot."

"I'm not stomping on your foot."

Grover clicks his tongue. "Shit. You're imaginary."

"I'm not imaginary."

"Then why won't you stomp on my foot?"

"Because I might hurt you."

"Physically, maybe. But that can heal. You can only hurt me *indefinitely* if you're imaginary," Grover says. He sticks out his foot. "Go ahead, I can take it."

"I'm not stomping on your foot," I say louder. "And you didn't answer my question. Do you think you're Grover Cleveland or you *are* Grover Cleveland?"

"I *am* Grover Cleveland."

"The president?"

"Technically, yes."

I put my head in my hands. "Oh God."

"No, *Grover*." He starts writing on the sheet of paper.

"What are you doing?" I ask, peeking through my hands and standing on my tiptoes to see what's on the page.

"Taking notes."

"On what?"

"You." Grover looks me up and down and starts writing again. "Black hair. Brown eyes. Appears to be around sixteen years old. Where are you from?"

"Arizona."

"Weird. I don't know anyone from Arizona," he says while writing.

"Why is that weird?"

"It's just interesting that my first hallucination would be from Arizona."

"I'm not a hallucination," I say again more emphatically.

Grover grins and says while writing, "Nice smile."

"You think I have a nice smile?"

"I don't know yet. You haven't smiled. It's a hypothesis. I plan on running multiple experiments to see if it is indeed a fact." He scribbles a few more things in his notebook. "Did you know that the odds of a person having true green eyes is one in fifty?"

"What?"

"It's true." Grover puts his pen in his mouth. "It'd be a damn shame if you're not real."

My cheeks heat and I look at the ground. "I told you. I'm real."

"We need someone to settle the debate. Come on." Grover grabs my arm and yanks me over to the tetherball courts next to the mess hall. A circle of kids watch as Cassie smacks a ball hooked to a string around the pole. She's smiling a wicked grin as she hits the ball repeatedly over a small boy's head. He can't be more than thirteen.

"Eat shit and die, fuckhead!" she screams when she wins. The little boy who she's playing against runs off the court, crying.

"Hey, Sticks!" Grover yells. "I need your help."

"Great." I yank my arm out of Grover's hand as Cassie comes over, her braless boobs bouncing under her shirt.

"What is it, Cleve?"

"You know each other?" I ask.

Cassie rolls her eyes and doesn't answer. "What can I help you with?"

Grover smiles and points at me. "Can you see her?"

"Unfortunately." Cassie pops her hip out to the side. "Zander's real, Cleve."

"Zander? She's real and has a name. It's nice to meet you, *Zander*." He holds out his hand for me to shake. I stare down at it, unsure if I really want to *meet* anyone at this camp. When I actually contemplate putting my hand in his, the tightness is back in my stomach. It's unwelcome and uncomfortable, so I push it down with a breath and wave at Grover instead. Just once.

"Well, now that we've determined you're real . . ." Grover rocks back on his heels, glancing down at his empty palm, before letting it fall. "What brings you to this fair part of Michigan, Zander?"

Cassie laughs. "Zander is here because 'her parents signed her up.'"

Grover puts the cap back on his pen. "Interesting."

"Aren't you going to make a note about that in your book?" I ask.

"I only write down the things I care never to forget."

"You carry a notebook around so that you won't forget things?"

"No," Grover says. "So I'll remember."

"Remember what?" I ask.

He takes a look around the camp and inhales like he's smelling a bouquet of flowers. "What it was like before."

Cassie moves to stand beside Grover. She actually looks like she cares about something for a moment. "Cleve is PC."

"PC?" I ask.

"Pre-Crazy," Grover says, shoving the notebook into his back pocket. "It'll happen one of these days."

"How do you know?"

"My dad converses with dead presidents."

"And they told him?" I ask.

Grover laughs, tipping his head back. "Some people get green eyes from their parents. Some people get schizophrenia. Clearly, I didn't get the green eyes."

"So the name . . ."

"My father's love for former presidents runs deep. Lucky for him, we had a fitting last name."

"But there's nothing wrong with you now. So why are you here?"

Grover sets his big blue-brown cartoon eyes on me. "Some people like to wait for the inevitable. I've never been much for waiting. What about you, Zander?"

I swallow the sudden lump in my throat. *Fini.* All done. The end is the end no matter when it happens. Waiting only makes it hurt more. A loose hair tickles the back of my neck, and I scratch the skin there a little too hard. "I hate waiting," I say.

"It only makes you hold on tighter." Grover's eyes stay strong on mine for a moment longer, and then he shoves his hands in his pockets. "If it's going to be my future, I might as well get used to it now. My dad was PC until he was sitting in a college history class and Teddy Roosevelt walked through the door. I figure if I'm lucky, I have a few more good years in me."

"How do you know Cassie?"

Grover wraps his arm around her neck. "Sticks and I have been coming here since eighth grade." He smiles at Cassie and whispers in her ear so softly that I can't hear a thing. Grover pats the front pocket of his jeans.

"What is it?" I ask.

"None of your concern." Cassie glares at me. "In the name of camp friendship, I should warn you, Cleve. Zander gives terrible blow jobs."

Grover reaches for his notebook, but I stop him. "No, I do not and don't write that down!"

He laughs. "I was just going to write that Zander looks cute when she blushes."

I grab my cheeks. "I'm not blushing."

"But you admit you've given a blow job?" Cassie asks.

I glare at her. "I have a boyfriend."

"That's a bummer," Grover says.

"His name is Coop."

"Double bummer. Don't tell me he plays football."

"He does," I say.

"So you're saying I should just give up now?"

I look into Grover's widened eyes as he watches me watching him. They reflect the sun, which makes them look like at any moment tears might come spilling out.

"Gag me," Cassie says as a bell rings. I jump at the sound.

"Why? When you've been doing such a fine job on your own," Grover says to Cassie, pointing to her too-skinny body. "Come on. My heightened emotional brain needs some food. Let's eat."

Grover moves toward the mess hall with Cassie close behind him. A mosquito bites my leg as I stand there. I swat it away and scratch the spot.

Grover glances over his shoulder and smiles. What am I waiting for?

If I have to deal with these bugs for five weeks, I'd better borrow some bug spray.

We go through the food line in the mess hall and I grab a set of silverware, which is wrapped together with a napkin, and a plastic tray. Food is spread out buffet-style on a long table, and I pick through the options. All the yellow food groups are covered—macaroni, chips, white bread, high-fructose corn syrup. My mom would be appalled. Coop complains every time he comes over to my house that my parents never have any food. My mom likes to correct him and say, "We have food in this house. You're just used to junk." Then she'll offer him a bowl of grapes or a granola bar.

I skip everything yellow and head for the salad bar at the end of the line. I fill my plate with as many colors of the rainbow as possible—green leaves, yellow peppers, red tomatoes, black olives, and, instead of salad dressing, a spoonful of cottage cheese. I even opt out of milk and settle on water, for hydration purposes.

When I pass a basket of apples at the end of the line, my feet stop in their place. I stare at the pile of fruit and pick one up, holding it close to my face. Its polished exterior shines in the dim yellow light of the mess hall, making its red skin look so edible. It's good for me, nutritionally speaking, and for a second, I even consider putting it on my tray.

"Wondering if you should eat the forbidden fruit?" Grover asks over my shoulder.

My eyes stay focused on it. "We never have apples in my house."

"Allergy?"

"No."

"Just a general dislike for the fruit?"

But I can't do it, no matter how good it might be for me to eat one. I set the apple down. The food line is backed up behind us. "Something like that," I say, and grab a whole-wheat roll instead. No butter.

Grover, Cassie, and I sit at an empty table. While Grover's tray has a heaping spoonful of macaroni and cheese and chicken fingers, Cassie has a measly serving of iceberg lettuce and five carrots.

"That lettuce has no nutritional value." I point at her tray. "It's practically all water."

"Do I look like I'm interested in nutritional value?" Cassie picks up one piece of lettuce and stuffs it in her mouth.

"I guess not," I say and start to break my roll into three pieces. When I was little, my mom taught me that three pieces is the polite thing to do. I'm not sure what's so impolite about two pieces or seven pieces or three million pieces for that matter, but my mom is a stickler for politeness and all things leafy and green. She holds on to these things like they're a life vest that can save her from drowning, but breaking her bread into three pieces won't save her. And when you hold on to things too tightly, they just rot in your grip.

I glance at the bin full of apples again. But not even my mom would be disappointed that I walked away from those.

"Zander," Grover says.

"What?"

"Hoping maybe the bread crumbs will lead you home?" He smiles and points down at my hands. I've shredded my roll into little tiny pieces that are now scattered all over the table. I scoop them up quickly and put them back on my tray.

I can't look at Grover when I say, "I don't want to go home."

When everyone has made it through the food line, the camp owner, Kerry, gets up at the front of the mess hall and silences everyone. "It's a camp tradition to pray to Saint Anthony of Padua, the patron saint of lost things, before our meal. Let's take a moment and bow our heads."

I look around the mess hall instead of following his directions. Every counselor has his or her head bowed. When Cassie picks up a knife and pretends to slit her throat, I utter a light laugh. I can't help it.

"We pray to Saint Anthony of Padua for three things. That the lost be found. That the soul be free. That life be everlasting."

"And that I get laid," Grover says. Kerry looks up with an annoyed expression on his face. "Isn't he the patron saint of lost things? I'm looking to lose my virginity."

"Please take this seriously," Kerry says.

"Believe me, I'm serious." Grover makes a cross over his heart.

"Let's eat." Kerry shakes his head and moves to sit down at a table with the other counselors.

"Nice one, Cleve," Cassie says, taking another bite of her lettuce.

"I can't help it. It's my heightened emotional state. Things come out of my mouth that shouldn't. Like that Zander has pretty eyes." Grover sets his fork down and looks at me. I mean really looks at me with the corner of his lips curled up.

"They're just brown. Lots of people have brown eyes."

"One in two people to be exact."

Cassie groans. "You won't lose anything to her. She said she has a boyfriend. All you'll get from her is a massive case of blue balls."

Grover's eyes don't leave mine. "Did someone say balls?" He winks. I look down at my plate with bread crumbs scattered all over as my cheeks heat. Coop doesn't make me blush. He doesn't make me anything other than better at French conjugations, and I like it that way.

I steal a look at Grover, uncomfortable with how little space is between us, when someone plops into the seat next to me. A short, fat kid with blunt blond hair cut straight across his forehead sits breathing heavily, his eyes wide on me.

"They're trying to kill me," he says.

"Who?" I ask.

"The counselors."

"Why?" Grover leans across the table toward the kid, intrigued.

The kid looks around the mess hall with wild eyes. He eases back in his seat. "Okay, they're not trying to kill me. But I heard they run secret experiments on campers in the middle of the night."

"Really?" I ask. The kid nods.

"That's why they lock us in." He pokes me in the shoulder and laughs. "I'm just kidding."

"What's your name, guy?" Grover gets out his notepad.

"Tim." The boy grabs a piece of bread from my tray and stuffs it in his mouth.

"Nice to meet you, Tim." Grover holds out his hand. "I take it because the ladies can see you, you're real. So what got you into this place?"

"I killed someone," Tim says with a mouthful of food, while he shakes Grover's hand. "And actually, the name's Pete."

"Who'd you kill, Pete?" Grover asks.

Pete takes my water and slugs down a gulp. "I'm just kidding. And actually, it's George."

"Okay, George." Grover makes a note. "Let me guess . . ." He puts his pen to his lips. "Compulsive liar?"

"I'm not a compulsive liar." The kid sits back in his seat, his brow knitted, and shakes his head. "Fine. Maybe I am. But I could be lying."

I glare at him, totally confused. "So what's your real name?"

Tim/Pete/George looks me square in the eyes. He can't be more than a freshman in high school, with rosy-red baby cheeks and pale skin that would burn if exposed to five minutes of sun unprotected, like me. "Alex Trebek."

"Like the old guy from *Jeopardy*?" I ask.

"That's not your fucking name," Cassie groans.

"Yes, it is."

"How do we know you're not lying?" I ask.

"I'm not lying."

"But you're a compulsive liar, so anything you say could be a lie," Grover says, tapping his pen on the side of the table.

"Maybe I'm lying about being a compulsive liar." Alex Trebek takes another swig of my water.

"Then that makes you a compulsive liar." Grover's eyes narrow, like he's thinking hard.

"But my name really is Alex Trebek."

Grover shakes his head. "But you could be lying about that."

"So basically, we can't trust a word you say," I cut in.

"Correct." Alex nods.

"But what if he's lying about that?" Grover points his finger at Alex and snaps. "Then that means we really *can* trust what he says."

"My head hurts." I bend down, pressing my forehead into the cool table.

Grover pats me on the back. "This is fascinating," he says and continues. But all I can pay attention to is Grover's hand on my back. It's hot through my clothes. When I can't take it anymore, I peel my head off the table and scoot my chair away from Grover.

Alex Trebek stays at our table for the rest of dinner. I eat a few bites of what's left of my bread and my salad. The spinach leaves a gross film on my teeth, but I don't touch my water because Alex drank half of it. With all this humidity, I'm not sure I actually need to drink water to stay hydrated anyway.

When everyone is finished eating, Kerry walks us through the camp's very extensive cleanup regimen. "Put your tray here. Dump any leftover food here. Stack plates here. Napkins go in the recycling bin. And hand your silverware to the counselor at the end of the line." Kerry points to the male counselor standing behind a table, a bus bin in front of him.

"Let me," Grover says, moving to stack all of our trays on top of his. Cassie and Alex Trebek, or whatever his real name is, hand theirs over willingly, but I keep mine.

"I'll do it."

"I don't mind." Grover smiles at me.

I clench the tray tighter. "No, thanks."

"A feminist. I like you even more, Zander."

Grover begins to clean up, but I keep my distance. I'm not sure what I expected from a camp like this, but so far, the first day has been beyond weird. Between Cassie, Alex, and Grover, I'm not sure where I fit. Nowhere probably, which is a good thing. If my parents just understood that *nowhere* is an actual place, it's just not the place they want me to be, everything would be okay. I'm fine there. Just fine.

Commotion erupts a few minutes later at the other end of the line, where the counselor is collecting silverware.

"There are only eight pieces here." The guy glares at Grover with an accusatory eye. "Where's the last piece?"

Grover shrugs but doesn't say a word. The longer he's silent, the more annoyed the counselor seems to get. I sit down and look at Cassie, who's lounging back in her seat like she's enjoying the show. Eventually Kerry walks over to assess the silverware situation. When he sees that Grover is the accused camper, he lets out a long, exaggerated breath.

"Where's the fork, Grover?"

"I don't know."

"Yes you do. You know exactly where it is."

"Kerry, you of all people should know that sometimes things go missing without any explanation. We just lose them. If that wasn't the case, I'd make sure never to lose my mind, but based on statistics, there's a pretty good chance one day it will up and leave me. My mind will be lost. Forever." Grover takes a breath. "Kind of like the fork."

Kerry rolls his eyes. "Where were you sitting?"

Grover leads him over to our table, the whole camp silently watching. I focus down at my hands as Kerry walks up to us.

"Cassie." Kerry lets out another huff. "I should have known."

"Known what?" she snaps.

"That you had something to do with this."

"Why are you so obsessed with silverware anyway?" Cassie asks.

"For starters, this camp isn't made of money." Kerry ticks things off on two fingers. "And secondly, as promised in the brochure, we ensure the safety of all of our campers. That includes counting the silverware. Now, where's the fork?"

"I don't know." Cassie looks off, seemingly undisturbed.

"Yes you do." Kerry's face swells with anger, the vein running down his forehead beginning to bulge.

Cassie glances back up at him, a serene look on her face that is starkly juxtaposed with Kerry's. "Pieces go missing all the time. The world is an imperfect place," she says.

Kerry clenches his jaw and moves his strong gaze to Alex Trebek.

Grover sits back in his seat, extending his legs under the table. "You won't get anything out of him. Particularly the truth."

"Do you know where the fork is?" Kerry asks Alex.

"What's a fork?"

Kerry groans. His eyes come to me next. "You're Zander, correct?"

"How did you know that?" I ask.

"I make it a point to know all of the campers." Kerry glances at Cassie out of the corner of his eye. "It's why we ask for a picture with your registration. Again, for safety reasons."

I sit back in my seat, feeling slightly betrayed. My parents sent Kerry a picture of me? What else did they tell him? I squirm in my seat, unsettled by the fact that a man who is a complete stranger probably knows things about me I don't want anyone to know. And it was my parents who told him.

"Do *you* know where the fork is, Zander?" Kerry asks.

"I . . ." I look from Grover to Alex to Cassie. She's sitting, lips puckered and arms crossed over her chest. I know Cassie has the fork and, at the same time, I know I don't want Kerry to get it back, just like I don't want Madison to teach me how to ride a horse or to paint my nails. Cassie narrows her eyes at me as if this is all just one big test. "I don't know what you're talking about," I say.

"Fine." Kerry looks back at Cassie. "*Someone* will just have to go without a fork for the rest of their stay."

Cassie scoffs. "Like I'd eat anything that requires a fork anyway."

When Kerry walks away from our table, Grover, Alex, Cassie, and I look at each other like we just got away with a crime. Grover's lips break into a large grin.

Kerry announces loudly to the rest of the campers that dinner is officially over.

"It's not easy searching for what we've lost," he says. "Especially when it's ourselves we have to find. Let's get some sleep. Those in need of medication, please meet at the Wellness Center."

Cassie gets up quickly and, without another word, walks out of the mess hall. She doesn't even bother saying thank-you to us for covering her ass.

"You look worried, Zander," Grover says, coming to stand next to me.

"I'm not worried."

"Good," he says.

Grover begins to walk away, but I stop him. "What if there's a fire? We're locked in."

"Don't worry," he says. "Physical constraints pale in comparison to mental ones. Now, repeat after me. We pray to Saint Anthony of Padua that the lost be found. That the soul be free. That life be everlasting."

CHAPTER 4

Aunt Chey,

My counselor is Madison. I hear she did it with a raw hot dog in high school. I hope she's reading this right now because I know she's standing behind me WATCHING ME WRITE THIS.

Kisses,

Cassie

The line at the Wellness Center for medication is long. Dori, Hannah, and Katie are all there. When I walk past, Dori stops me. She's holding a small Dixie Cup.

"You don't take anything?" she asks.

"No."

Dori shakes her head. "That's right. You're here because your 'parents signed you up.'" She rolls her eyes as she shoots her pills like a shot of liquor.

"It's Prozac," Hannah says, showing me what's inside her cup.

Cassie walks up next to us. "Boring." She stretches out the word. "Everyone's on Prozac."

"What about you?" I ask her. "No meds?"

"You think I'd let any doctors come close to me? They won't give me what I want. Plus, I've got all the medicine I need." She starts to walk away, but I grab her arm to stop her.

"Where's the fork?"

Cassie pulls away from my grip but doesn't respond. She shakes her head as she leaves, her skinny legs even skinnier in the twilight.

At the cabin, we brush our teeth and get dressed for bed. Dori takes the bunk above my bed, and Cassie is on the lower bunk next to me with Hannah on top. Katie is the sucker who has to share a bunk with Madison. I glance at the duffel bag stuffed under Cassie's bed filled with her "medication."

"Lights out in fifteen minutes, girls," Madison says. "Sleep is important."

I lie in bed, on top of the single sheet, and flip through the *Seventeen* magazine I picked up at the airport on the way here. I bought it so my dad wouldn't talk to me on the flight, but I didn't actually read any of the articles. For each page, I counted to one hundred in my head and then flipped it. It worked. My dad listened to a podcast on his phone the entire flight, and I got the solitude of counting in my head.

Just me . . . the thought makes me remember the quilt stuffed in my bag, and I have to choke down the bile that rises in my throat.

I focus back on the magazine. The dim light of the sunset creeps through the window above my bed, but even then it's hard to see the words on the page. Both Hannah and Katie plug their ears with headphones and turn up the music so loud I can hear the heavy beat. The camp doesn't allow any cell phones. When my parents told me that, it was a relief. A summer without a single call from my mom sounded nice.

She is a compulsive texter.

`Did u remember to grab the lunch I packed u?`

`I made u a hair appointment for Friday.`

`Let's practice driving after school.`

`I'm making lasagna for dinner.`

`Drink at least 64 ounces of water today.`

`The sun will set at 5:45.`

At one point this past year, it got so bad that my English teacher took my phone away and carted me down to the office. Mr. Ortiz said he couldn't teach with all the dinging.

He even called my mom *with* my phone. She apologized and actually cried. I could hear her sobs through the receiver. Mr. Ortiz felt so bad that he gave me back my phone and said if it ever died, I could use the one in the English office. Then he apologized for saying the word *died.*

"I mean—if it ever runs out of batteries," he corrected himself.

The no-phone rule was the only fight my parents had about Camp Padua. My mom yelled so loudly about how unfair it is that I can't have one, I could hear her shrieking voice in my room with the door closed, and then she threw something against the wall. By the time I came down to dinner, whatever she had smashed had been cleaned up. My mom made portobello vegan stroganoff, and my dad said it was his favorite thing she'd cooked in at least a year. The Camp Padua brochure never moved from underneath the magnet on our refrigerator.

The lead article on the cover of the magazine is "How to Flirt without Being Obvious." I glare at the words until they get fuzzy and then the buzzing begins. The small sound of a mosquito moves in and out of my ears, like it's circling my head. I roll up the magazine, holding it in my hand like a club, and sit up. When I see the mosquito land on my white sheet, I bring the magazine down on it hard, squashing the bug into the cotton. I flick the dead thing onto the ground.

"Oh sure," Cassie says, "your parents just signed you up." She swirls her finger around her temple and rolls over in bed so she's facing the wall. The rest of the girls laugh in unison.

I face the opposite direction of Cassie, wanting as much distance between us as possible. I don't care that we ate at the same table. I want nothing to do with her. I want nothing to do with anyone at this camp or anyone out of this camp for that matter.

The silver lock on the cabin door glimmers in the dull light coming through the windows. But I'm locked in, forced to be with these people. I place the *Seventeen* magazine over my face, and, lying back on top of my sheet, start to conjugate words in the French *imparfait.*

To speak:

Je parlais

Tu parlais

Il parlait

Nous parlions

Vous parliez

Ils parlaient

I lie still, drifting further away from reality and feeling the ease of sleep come over me. Sleep is so pleasant. I can drift into the blackness and no one cares. It's expected.

I'm gone for only a bit when a tapping feeling starts in my light sleep, like water is dripping on my head from a leak in the ceiling. I wipe the feeling away, annoyed, and roll over.

The sound of my magazine falling on the ground triggers something in my subconscious that remembers a ceiling isn't over my head.

Dori's bed is. And it's back. The dripping or tapping. I sit up in the dark, almost banging my head on the bunk. Cassie is inches away from my face, her dark eyes big, the whites practically glowing.

"What are you doing?" I ask, scooting back. It's dark now in the cabin, but still I can see that Cassie looks crazier than usual.

"I'm waking you up so you can help me, asshole," she says.

"Why would I want to help you? You just called me an asshole."

"Because you don't like that lock as much as I do." Cassie points to the door.

I sit back on the bed. Madison is tucked neatly under her quilt, her mouth slightly open with the smallest bit of drool on her pillow. The key still hangs around her slender neck. I must have been asleep longer than I thought.

"Are you gonna help me or what, moron?"

"Don't call me a moron," I say. "I got an A plus in French."

Cassie rolls her eyes. "Listen, I'm about one minute away from strangling Madison with her necklace. So either you help me get out of here or you become an accomplice to murder."

"I'm going back to sleep." I lie down.

"Suit yourself," Cassie says. She moves to stand over Madison's bed and pulls something pointed and sharp out of her back pocket.

"Are you crazy?" I whisper, shooting up.

"Of course, I'm crazy. And so are you, even if you don't want to admit it. There's a secret inside of you, Zander. And it's coming out this summer whether you like it or not." Cassie squats in front of me. Her face is so close to mine, I can smell her sugary breath. There's even a hint of lemon. I want to shove her away from me. Who is she to comment on my life? Cassie doesn't even know me. But I can't bring myself to touch her, because a part of me knows she's right. "You know what your problem is? You're not actually afraid of me. You're afraid you *are* me," she says.

"No." I struggle with the word like I'm physically fighting with the truth. The longer and harder I press it down, the more it pushes back. "I'm just afraid you're going to kill Madison with whatever you have in your hand."

"Don't you ever just want to kill someone because you're that angry?"

I can't answer Cassie because it's a ridiculous question, but a lump forms in my throat anyway. It's so big I might choke. I swallow it, pushing it back down, and breathe in her oddly sweet breath. Cassie holds up the pointy object. "It's just a fork, asshole. What am I going to do, poke her to death?"

"I knew you took it."

"Duh." Cassie rolls her eyes. "Who cares? It's a fork. People eat too much anyway."

I ease back on the bed. "How are you planning to get out? What about Madison?"

"What *about* Madison? I wouldn't touch her with a ten-foot pole covered in slime. The slime would get a bacteria."

"The key." I point to her neck.

"That's your problem. You think a key will get us out of this. A key can't do anything for you or me."

"Fine, then what will get you out?" I ask.

"You." Cassie points to the bathroom door. "My aunt always says that when God closes the door, somewhere he opens a window."

"I think that's from a movie." Or one of the magnets hanging on my fridge.

"I don't care where it's from," Cassie says. "And I don't actually believe it. As far as I'm concerned all windows and doors just lead to more windows and doors."

"So there's no way out of anything?" I ask.

"Sure there is," Cassie says. "Death is the way out."

"Death." I don't move as I say the word. Cassie's shadow moves the moonlight's glow on my single white sheet as she nods.

"Now, are you gonna help me or what?"

"I don't think sneaking out is a good idea."

"And what *is* a good idea?" she asks.

I fumble for too long. "I don't know," I say.

"That's your other problem. You *don't* know." She shakes her head and stifles a laugh. "God, Cleve is so wrong about you."

"What did Grover say?"

"His name is *Cleve*." Cassie puts the fork in her back pocket. "And time's ticking. I'm out of here."

She tiptoes into the bathroom. I lie back down in bed and pull my single sheet up around my neck. If Cassie wants to sneak out, she can do it herself. I'm not her accomplice or confidant or friend. I'm nothing to her and I want it to stay that way.

And then before I know it, I've twisted a small patch of hair at the base of my neck too tight around my finger until a few strands pop free.

"Damn it," I whisper, looking down at the loose pieces. It will take years for that hair to grow back out. I never learn my lesson. I just need to let my hair be, to stop pulling so hard at it. That's what I've been trying to do for the past year. Just let everything be, but my parents don't understand that. They want me to be something because something is better than nothing. I disagree. We all end up as nothing in the end anyway. But with Cassie in my face and Grover touching me today, those two make it hard to ignore them. I ball up the pathetic strands of hair and sprinkle them on the ground.

I try distracting myself with my magazine, but I can't stand to look at the model on the cover with her long, thick perfect hair. So I rip the cover off. I rip it again and again and again until all that's left are little broken pieces of paper that could never be put back together. I dust them off my bed, smiling.

In the bathroom, I find Cassie using her fork to unhinge the window. A long screw falls free into her hand, and the window loosens enough to fit a teenage body. Especially one of a girl who doesn't eat.

Cassie hands me the screw. "Keep it safe."

"I don't want it." But I don't hand it back.

When Cassie is safely outside, I hear her say, "Tell anyone about this and I'll be forced to use my fork on you."

I don't close the window on her. Instead, I stuff the screw in my bag and go back to sleep.

CHAPTER 5

Dear Mom and Dad,

Please send bug spray. You forgot to pack some. See—even parents make mistakes.

Z

"Do they serve coffee here?" Dori asks Madison as we go down the breakfast line in the mess hall. "I need coffee."

"No substances with physically or mentally altering chemicals," Madison says, like she's reading straight from the brochure again.

"Coffee isn't a chemical. It's life support."

Cassie was in bed when I woke up this morning, her leg dangling over the edge of the bottom bunk. I was relieved and then frustrated that I cared, so I lay there staring up at the top bunk, daydreaming about my boring two-story stucco home that always smells like grapefruit-scented cleaner. But the longer I lay there, the quieter the cabin became and the more I wanted someone to make some noise again. Luckily, Cassie woke up a few minutes later and picked a fight with Madison that ended with Cassie threatening to tell her Aunt Chey that she contracted crabs at camp.

"We're going to work on *you* being your own life support," Madison says, grabbing Dori's shoulders, like a coach giving a pep talk. I sprinkle a few berries on my oatmeal and yawn into my hand. The more they talk, the more my ears begin to hum.

"Well, this machine must be broken. Because it needs coffee to stay alive," Dori says.

"That's why I'm here. To help you fix your broken machine." Madison smiles.

"Life support only keeps you alive," I say softly over my shoulder. "It doesn't help you live."

"And what's wrong with being broken? Are you perfect or something?" Dori asks Madison.

"No," Madison says, slightly taken aback. "Of course not."

Grover and Alex Trebek sit in the same spot as yesterday. I hesitate going to the table for a second, but sitting anywhere else at this point seems useless. Something tells me it would only incite more attention from Grover and Cassie anyway.

I set my stuff down next to Grover and pull on the thick straps of my too-tight bathing suit under my clothes. Grover picks up an apple from his tray and tosses it in the air to me. I barely manage to catch it before it falls on the table.

"Did you know that apple seeds are poison?" Grover asks.

"Really," I say flatly.

"One apple won't kill you. You have to eat, like, a whole bunch of apples."

I set it back on his tray. "Interesting."

Grover gives the apple back to me. "This is for you."

"Are you trying to poison me?"

"I just told you, one apple wouldn't kill you."

"I don't want it," I say.

"I know you said you don't like them, but you don't have to be afraid."

"I said I don't want it," I bark at him and shift uncomfortably in my seat. Why did my mom pack this suit?

The tension between us doesn't break until Cassie sits down.

"I can see you're having your usual breakfast. Air and diet pills," Grover says to Cassie.

"No fork needed." Cassie smiles, but it doesn't reach her eyes.

Grover passes her something that rattles and sounds suspiciously like pills behind my back.

"I can't believe you'd actually give her that," I say.

"It's not what you—" Cassie starts, but Grover cuts her off.

"Why not? It makes her happy. And she needs more happiness in her life."

"But it hurts her."

"Only a little. And everything that makes us happy will eventually hurt us," Grover counters.

"I just thought you cared about her." I look down at my bowl of oatmeal.

"I *do* care about her," Grover says.

"Then how could you give her more pills?"

Cassie laughs and holds up what Grover gave her. "It's candy, moron." She shakes a box of Lemonheads at me.

"Candy?" I ask.

"I have to eat something to stay alive," she says.

"Candy." I glare at Grover. A puckered smile sits on his face.

"I never eat," Alex Trebek says. His round cheeks are extra puffy with the smile on his face. He takes a bite from the mound of scrambled eggs on his tray. "Never," he says with a mouth full of food.

"Nice one, Bek." Grover pats him on the back.

"Why is the liar sitting with us again?" Cassie groans.

"Because he told me he's dying of cancer. He only has a few days to live. I feel bad for him."

Cassie dumps the entire box of Lemonheads in her mouth. I can smell the sugar from across the table.

"Don't you ever get sick of those?" I ask. "They're so sweet."

Cassie leans toward me with full cheeks. "They're the only sweet thing in my life. So no, I don't get sick of them."

"Fine." I poke at my oatmeal and take a few bites, but I'm not hungry.

When all of us are finished eating, Kerry stands at the front of the group and claps three times. "The only way to be found," he yells.

"Is to admit we're lost," the rest of the counselors say back to him.

"The first step in finding yourself is acknowledging what you already have," Kerry says loudly. For such an early morning, he's finely groomed in a sexy kind of way. I didn't notice that yesterday. I was too focused on his face vein. "Before we start our day, would anyone like to acknowledge something this morning?"

No one moves. I stare down and twist my napkin around my finger until the finger turns blue. I yawn. Out of the corner of my eye, I see Grover raise his hand and stand.

"I'd like to acknowledge that Zander doesn't eat apples," he says.

"What?" I look up at him.

"I meant acknowledge something about yourself," Kerry says.

"Oh." Grover nods. "Then I acknowledge me acknowledging that Zander doesn't eat apples."

I gasp at him and stand up. "I'd like to acknowledge that it's none of Grover's business what I eat."

"I'd like to acknowledge that that's probably true." Grover nods.

"Thank you." I begin to sit down.

"But." When Grover starts to speak again, I stay still. "I'd like to acknowledge that just because I've acknowledged that it's none of my business doesn't mean that I haven't acknowledged that Zander doesn't eat apples."

"Please set an example and take this seriously, Grover," Kerry says.

"I *am* being serious. What I think you mean to say is please make this about me. But I'm much more interested in Zander."

"That's avoidance of your problems." Kerry crosses his arms over his chest. "You know this, Grover."

"Yes. It is. But problems are depressing and there's enough depression around here."

"Amen," Cassie pipes up.

"I think we're done with this exercise, since you're clearly not going to benefit from it." Kerry begins to sit down.

"But Zander might," Grover says.

"Leave me out of it," I say loudly.

"Too late." Grover shrugs. "It's already been acknowledged."

I plop down in my seat, my napkin balled between my fingers.

"Thank you, Grover," Kerry says, unenthusiastically.

"One more thing." Grover sticks up his pointer finger and gets out his notebook. He starts writing. "So I remember. I'd also like to acknowledge that Zander is wearing a black bathing suit and I'd like to see her in it. Whether she eats apples or not."

"Boy-girl relationships are not allowed at camp." Kerry repeats one of his rules like a robot.

"Well, then I'd like to acknowledge the stupidity of that rule. Plus, Zander and Grover sounds like a gay couple."

"Okay." Kerry shakes his head.

Bek raises his hand and stands next to Grover. "I'd like to acknowledge that Cassie is pretty and I want to see her naked. Forget the bathing suit." His voice is loud and kind of shaky as he stares across the table at Cassie, his blue eyes shining.

"Is he lying, Cleve?" she barks with wide eyes.

Grover shrugs. "I can't tell."

"Sit your fat ass down, Porky," Cassie says.

"Anything you say, beautiful," Bek says and winks.

I stay frozen in my seat, even after Kerry gives up on the morning's exercise. I wish I was numb, but I'm humming, vibrating, practically shaking in my chair. As Grover collects his things, he leans over to me and sets the apple he's eaten to the core on my tray. "Sorry about the bathing suit comment, but I had to say it. Heightened emotional state and all."

I can't look at him.

"I'm an ass. I acknowledge that. And I've got problems," he says, touching my shoulder.

"No touching," I bark.

"You know one in two people will contract an STD in their lifetime, but the likelihood of getting one through touching is, like, zero."

I storm away without a word, but before I leave the mess hall, I grab a packet of sugar from the food line. I glare down at my barely eaten bowl of oatmeal that tasted like little flakes of cardboard.

Oatmeal is a heart-healthy meal. My mom's voice rings in my ears. *Don't ruin it by dumping pure junk on top.*

But Cassie is right about sweet things. I rip open the sugar packet and shake the whole thing into my mouth. Then I eat another one. Then I think I might puke. Then I think someone will peg me for a purger and I choke it down.

And as I hold the empty packets in my hand, I can't believe I just acknowledged that Cassie was right about something.

"Every time you come to the beach, you are required to hang your metal circle on this board, so the counselor on duty can know who is in the water and what their ability levels are. Each of you will be given a different color." Madison stands in front of a large wooden board with the words At Camp Padua There's FUN in FUNdamentals written across the top. The board is covered in hooks and divided into three different-colored sections: red, yellow, and green. She swings a whistle around her fingers as she talks. "If you're a red, you must wear a life jacket and stay within the shallow end of the H dock." Madison points to the section closest to shore that is enclosed by three sides of the metal dock. "The life jackets are in the equipment shed. If you're a yellow, you can go out as far as the end of the dock, which is marked by that line of buoys. If you're a green, you can go as far out as the raft just offshore. That is the end of Camp Padua property."

The raft Madison is referring to is square with a ladder and floats a little distance away from the H dock. It probably fits about five people tops.

I look out at the green water. Other than the few steps I took into Lake Kimball yesterday, I haven't been in a large body of water since I was asked to leave our high school's swim team last year. The water is smooth again today—just small, insignificant waves coming to shore. I count them as they lap against the sand.

"Zander," Madison says.

"Huh?" I snap back to her.

"This is important." She continues to drone on about the test. "It consists of a stroke check, a five-minute tread, and a diving test." Madison finally smiles and says, "I'm sure you'll all do great. Let's get started!"

We strip down to our suits, each of us glancing at each other, one more self-conscious than the next, except for Cassie who looks too comfortable taking off her clothes. It gets even weirder when Hannah leaves her long-sleeved shirt on.

"I don't want to get burnt," she says, even though her skin is caramel colored and I doubt the sun has ever done any damage other than giving her a nice brown glow. I cringe, guessing she's more worried about exposing the damage she's inflicted to herself.

We wait by the edge of the lake as Cassie sits down on her towel in her hot-pink bikini and leans her face back into the sun.

"Cassie, would you please join us?" Madison says.

"I'm not taking the test." Cassie's face doesn't move from looking skyward.

"Then I'll be forced to give you level red. I don't want to do that."

"Like you care. And like I'm gonna go in that water anyway. There are probably leeches in there."

"I do care and there aren't leeches," Madison says.

"Well, I'd rather work on my tan."

"Your tan?" Madison tries to keep the sarcasm out of her voice. Cassie is darker than all of us combined. "Fine. If that's how you want it, I won't force you. It's your decision." Madison gets a red washer out of a bag and throws it down on Cassie's towel with a black permanent marker. "Please write down your name and hang it on the wooden board. The rest of you can get started."

My toes squish into the sand as we walk out to waist-deep water, but it feels good. The air is warm and soggy today, like a damp sponge. I skim my hands over the water and feel the liquid course between my fingers.

"For the stroke test, you must swim from dock to dock twice in the red zone with any stroke you choose. Pick your strongest stroke," Madison says.

When I submerge my head in the cold water, my breath gets tight adjusting to the temperature. It's like jumping into my school's barely heated pool at five thirty every morning for two months. I feel like I'm right back on the varsity swim team. But when I open my eyes under water, all that's around me is green and brown. The water is so murky, I can barely see in front of me.

I glide doing the breaststroke, using as little energy as I can. When I feel the dock, I flip underwater to switch directions. I lag a bit on my turn. My coach would be disappointed my turns are not the speed they used to be.

"Nice job," Madison says when I'm done.

Next is the five-minute tread.

"You must stay afloat for five minutes, your entire face never going below the surface of the water. If you get tired, come to the dock. Don't risk it," Madison says.

I float on my back, looking up at the sun, my legs kicking lightly in the water as my arms flap like wings at my side.

That's what I always liked about swimming. The way I could get lost in the rhythm. I won every meet by doing that. Every meet until the last one. After that, my dad hung the Camp Padua brochure under one of my mom's inspirational magnets on the fridge. I walked past it every morning and evening on my way to and from school. One day, I actually stood right in front of it and looked at the smiling faces of the campers posed on the cover.

"What's that?" Coop asked, chomping on the kale chips my mom made earlier that day. "These taste like ass."

I touched the glossy paper and almost picked it up, but every few seconds my eyes would drift to the magnet with the word Hope written on it in script. What a ridiculous word. I made out with Coop on the couch instead of reading the brochure. He didn't taste like ass from the kale chips, more like a weed.

I close my eyes as the memories come back to me and my chin starts to dip under the water.

My dad cried when I got kicked off the swim team. He begged the coach to let me stay on. He said that I would do better, that I wouldn't put myself or the team at risk again, but those were his words, not mine. Life is a risk. In the end, my coach said I was a liability.

My dad yelled at me when we got home from the meet, though I'm not sure what he said, I was so lost in French conjugations. When he raised his hand to smack me, my mom grabbed his arm. That's when my dad started crying. He fell to his knees and hugged me around the waist. My hair was still wet and making the back of my shirt cold, so when he finally let go, I went to the bathroom to blow-dry my hair.

To hope in French: *espérer.*

I look up at the sky, my mouth so close to the surface of the water I can taste it. A muffled ringing sound brings me out of my trance.

Dori, Katie, and Hannah hold on to the dock as Madison waves her arm calling me back to them.

"Nice job, Zander," Madison says again. My coach would always say that, too. *Nice job, Zander.* And he'd pat me on the head like a dog.

"I think I'm done," Hannah says, pulling herself out of the water.

"Are you sure? You were doing so well," Madison offers.

"I don't plan on swimming a lot this summer anyway," Hannah says and takes a yellow washer.

Madison looks disappointed as Hannah leaves the dock to sit by Cassie on the beach.

"Okay, ladies, the diving test is next. You must swim to the bottom of the lake, find one of the diving sticks, and bring it back to me on the dock. It's about twelve feet, so if you feel like you're not going to make it, do not hesitate to come back to the surface. We'll do this one at a time. Who would like to go first?"

Dori and Katie both take their turns and are successful bringing the yellow diving stick to the surface. When Madison calls on me, I stand, my toes curled over the end of the H dock as she tosses a yellow stick into the water.

My hands hit the water, like slicing ice. The coolness travels down my body, and the deeper I get into Lake Kimball the colder it feels. The yellow stick sits in the sand and I grab it, but stop. I float inches from the bottom, my hand skimming the sand. It's smooth and falls through my fingers, and I think I could stay here where things just float through time sink to the bottom.

When my lungs start to squeeze as my breath runs out, I slam my feet on the sand and come back to the surface.

"Zander!" Madison yells from the end of the dock. She looks like she's about to jump in. "I thought you weren't going to make it for a second. You scared me."

I give her the yellow diving stick. "Sorry."

"Kerry said your parents told him you had an issue with swimming."

"My parents told him that?" I ask. Madison nods. I can tell the concern on her face is real and it only makes me angrier. I don't want her concern or pity.

I don't respond. I write my name on the green washer she hands me and hang it on the board. *Fini.*

CHAPTER 6

Cher Papa,
Je pense que j'ai un cancer.
Cordialement,
Alex Trebek

My hair is still damp and the littlest bit of water clogs my ear as I head toward the archery field. I jump on one leg to get it out as I walk up to the group of campers circling counselor Hayes. I was surprised when Madison showed me the archery field. It seemed a little dangerous considering the camp's clientele. I have a cabin mate who likes to inflict bodily harm on *herself.* And Kerry threw a fit over a fork last night.

"With safety we have more fun," Hayes says, holding up the archery equipment. Turns out that the bows and arrows in his hands are plastic. The kind little kids play with. No pointy arrowheads, only suction cups.

"Figures," I mumble to myself. I raise my hand to ask if there's enough time to change activities.

"Yes, Durga, how can I help you?" Hayes holds out an archery set and smiles. He has a full head of black dreadlocks and is as dark as Cassie. One of the dreads even has a jangling bell hanging from the end.

"Durga? My name is Zander."

Hayes smiles. "Durga is an awesome Hindu warrior goddess. She defeated the mighty Mahishasura when all the other *men* couldn't. You look like you might have a little warrior in you."

I take the bows and arrows, unsure of what to say. I don't feel like a warrior, Hindu or otherwise; I feel tired, but it's too late to leave now.

"Archery is about precision and patience." Hayes blinks slowly. "Kind of like life. We breathe in and aim. Then we breathe out and release. We take our time. It isn't about hitting the target so much as the path that leads us to the target. As life would be, after you hit one target, there's always another one in front of you." Hayes exhales all the breath out from his lungs and smiles. "Let's breathe together."

The group of campers takes a deep breath.

"That was a start. Now let's try it again. When we breathe together, we become a part of something larger than ourselves. Support your neighbor and let them support you," Hayes says. "It's the journey, not the destination."

We take another deep breath and another.

"Inhale. Aim. Exhale. Release. Hit your target. Enjoy the journey." He lifts and lowers his arms through the air, gesturing for every breath we take. "Great. Now, let's practice. Just with your bows. Remember to keep breathing. That's a lesson for everything in life. Just keep breathing."

Just keep breathing. Please. That's all I ask. The words pull on my body as my mom's voice rings in my ear. I don't want her here with me. I just want to be alone with the humming in my head, like a warm blanket that protects me from cold weather. A blanket I can pull all the way over me and disappear.

"You're still wearing your bathing suit."

I turn to find Grover next to me. I lose my focus and drop my bow.

"What are you doing here?" I ask.

"Bek insisted." Grover gestures to the other side of the group where Bek is practicing aiming and breathing. "You're still wearing your bathing suit," he says again.

I don't respond, but tug on my shirt so it's not so clingy.

"Are you not answering because you're still mad at me?" he asks.

"I'm not mad. You made a statement. I don't have to respond."

"You're smart, aren't you?" Grover tries to nudge my shoulder but I dodge his touch.

"It doesn't matter."

"Everything matters." Grover squints at me. "Is this because of your boyfriend who plays football?"

"No," I say, suddenly protective even though I don't care much about Coop at all. If he was having sex right now with Miley Ryder, the most popular girl in our grade, I'd probably be more upset that my French grade might drop from a lack of conjugating during kissing than that he's cheating on me.

Hayes walks up to us. "Are you breathing together?" he asks.

"Always." Grover wiggles his eyebrows. He licks the suction cup end of his arrow and sticks it on my arm. "Aim. Release. Hit your target."

I stare down at the arrow that's covered in Grover's spit. It's warm and kind of gross . . . but kind of not.

I pull the arrow free. "Gross," I say and toss it at him.

Hayes has us line up in front of the plastic targets and practice. Grover doesn't leave my side, and my ear won't drain, the echo totally distracting. I stick my finger in my ear and jump up and down. I shake my head. Nothing works.

"God, you're sexy," Grover says when I flip my head over and hop on one foot.

"You have problems."

"I acknowledge that."

"Don't say that again," I groan.

"Okay. But just so you know I acknowledge that."

We practice aiming and releasing, most of us missing the target over and over again. At one point, Grover throws down his bow and yells, "This is impossible! I can't clear my brain. In the past ten seconds, I've thought about seven different kinds of sandwiches and what Zander would look like eating them."

"Stop thinking about me," I say, my voice reverberating in my head. But the water stays.

"That would be impossible."

Hayes picks up Grover's bow and hands it to him. "Just breathe," he says.

I look around at the other campers, who can't seem to hit the target any better than Grover and I, when I catch Bek nail a bull's-eye with his plastic arrow. And then somehow he does it again.

I get so entranced by Bek and his ability that I forget about the water in my ear and that Grover thinks about sandwiches and me eating them. Bek's eyes never leave the target in front of him. He holds the bow up to his cheek, pulls back, inhales, and before he exhales and releases, I watch him say something to himself. He lands another bull's-eye effortlessly.

I move closer to him to hear what he's saying, but it's mumbled and I only catch a little bit because of the damn water in my ear. I jump on my one side, trying to shake it out. Warmth hits my earlobe as the clog finally lets go and Bek's words ring clear.

"You're speaking French," I say. Bek startles at the sound of my voice and drops his bow on the ground.

"No."

"You're lying."

"Maybe."

"So what's your secret?" I ask him.

"I don't have a secret."

"Yes, you do. I heard you. You said, *Voici mon secret.*"

"You know French?" When I nod, Bek says, "I don't have a secret."

"Then why did you say that?" I ask.

He picks up his bow. "Fine, you caught me. I do have a secret. I have X-ray vision. Nice bathing suit by the way. Grover will be jealous that I saw it first."

I hug my chest, even though I know he's lying. "What were you really saying?"

"I don't know what you're talking about. I don't even speak French." Sweat peeks out on Bek's forehead beneath his blond hair as the lunch bell rings.

"Looks like it's about time for food. Please bring all equipment back to me," Hayes says.

"Voici mon secret," I say to myself as I watch Bek walk across the field toward the mess hall. "Here is my secret."

"What secret?" Grover asks, coming to stand next to me.

"Nothing."

"That's not true." Grover says and winks at me. "It's always something."

"Don't think of this as therapy. Think of it as . . . *share*-apy," Madison says as we sit around the Circle of Hope. "This is an open forum for you to share with us about your life. I'm here to support you without judgment." A small figurine sits on Madison's lap as she gestures to the group.

We sit around the Circle of Hope: a bulimic, a cutter, a depressed teenager, a self-diagnosed manic-depressive-bipolar-anorexic disaster who some days thinks she's a boy locked in a girl's body, Madison, and me.

"Is that what Kerry taught you in camp training?" Cassie scoffs.

"Yes." Madison nods. "Actually, he did."

"Is he even qualified to train you?"

"Kerry holds a doctorate degree in psychology and social work. He's written numerous articles about his work at the camp. He's kind of a genius."

Cassie's eyes light up. "You want to screw him, don't you?"

Madison goes stiff but doesn't respond to the comment. Instead, she holds up the figurine. "This is Saint Anthony of Padua. He'll be our 'talking stick.' We'll pass him to whoever is sharing as a reminder that it's their turn to talk. It's our job to listen."

I dig my foot into the ground and move the dirt around with the toe of my shoe. I don't plan on talking. I've done too much of it lately and swimming and participating. Right now, I'd just like a nap. An uncontrollable yawning fit comes over me as we sit waiting for anyone to start.

"Okay, I'll go," Madison says. "I grew up in Birmingham just a few hours away from here. I'm getting my masters in social work at Michigan State, and my undergrad is in psychology with a minor in English."

Cassie yawns in unison with me. "That's not sharing. That's bragging. Get some real problems, Mads," she says.

"Please don't call me Mads."

"Okay, Mads," Cassie says.

Madison straightens out and offers St. Anthony to Cassie. "Why don't you share next?"

Cassie crosses her arms over her chest. "I don't have anything to brag about."

"Someone else?" Madison looks around the circle. "Dori, what about you?"

Dori glances around at us and reluctantly takes the figurine. "I'm fifteen years old. I'm from Chicago. My mom and dad are divorced and I live with my mom."

"That's good." Madison nods.

"It's actually not that good. I hate my stepdad."

"I just meant that it's good of you to share."

"Well, it isn't good. It sucks." Dori plays with the bottom of her shirt, rolling St. Anthony in the fabric.

"Why don't you tell us why it sucks?" Madison leans in.

"I don't know." Dori's eyes won't come off her shirt. "My stepdad is an ass. My mom pays more attention to him than to me. And I wish I could live with my dad, but he moved to Oregon to be with his new wife."

"How does that make you feel?"

"Forget it," Dori mumbles, but Madison doesn't move on. We all wait for Dori to say more. "I guess I should be happy for my parents but I'm not."

Madison pats her knee. "Don't *should* on yourself, Dori."

"Don't *should* on yourself?" Cassie breaks the moment and bursts into hysterics. "Did you just say that for real?"

"I don't want this anymore." Dori shoves the St. Anthony figurine into Madison's hand and stares down at the ground like maybe a hole will suddenly appear and swallow her.

Madison looks at Cassie with a tight face.

"Don't look at me, Mads. You're the one who's talking about people shitting on themselves."

"*Shoulding* on themselves," Madison corrects. "Saying how you *should* feel is counterproductive to dealing with how you *do* feel."

Cassie rolls her eyes, but Madison directs her attention back at Dori. "I hear what you're saying. I remember when my parents got divorced. It sucked."

"Your parents are divorced?" Dori perks up as Madison nods.

"Okay. Who would like to go next?" Madison asks.

Hannah and Katie share that they're both from Indiana, but not the same town. Katie's parents are divorced, too, but she likes her stepdad better than her real dad. The whole time the girls talk, Cassie laughs or makes grunting noises and continually rolls her eyes.

"Cassie, would you please stop doing that," Madison says.

"Me? I'm not the problem here."

"Well, then what is the problem?"

Cassie narrows her eyes as the air around the circle gets heavy. It's as if a cloud rolls over us and brings the temperature down to a chill.

"Why don't you ask Katie what you really want to know?" Cassie says.

"I just want to know her," Madison replies. "The real her. That's what we're trying to focus on this first week: Knowing ourselves. Our *true* selves."

"You just want to know why she stuffs her fingers down her throat. And then you want to pat yourself on the back for making Katie admit to things that are none of your business."

"That's not true," Madison says. She holds out St. Anthony to Cassie. "Why don't you share with us what you're hoping to find?"

Cassie snatches the figurine out of Madison's hands in a quick move that surprises everyone. "What am I hoping to find?" she scoffs. "What are *you* hoping to find here, Madison? A venereal disease?"

"That's enough, Cassie." Madison reaches out to take the figurine back.

"No." She pulls away. "All we are is a line on your perfect resume. You don't want to help us. We are your science experiment, so you can go back to college and brag about how you helped lost teenagers this summer while banging a guy with occasional body odor and hair longer than yours."

"That's not true."

"I'll tell you what is true." Cassie turns to the group and points. "Katie makes herself puke because society tells her she's fat and she doesn't love herself enough not to care. Dori hates her stepdad because her real dad abandoned her for another woman. And I gotta admit. That one must sting."

"That's enough, Cassie. Please sit down," Madison says.

"Hannah cuts herself because she'd rather feel physical pain than admit to her emotional pain. Though I'm not sure what it is that hurt her so bad. And Zander might be the most fucked-up of us all because she won't admit to anything."

I freeze when I hear my name. "What?" I ask.

"That's right, Z, you're more fucked-up than me." Cassie gives me a wild grin and holds out St. Anthony. "Why don't you tell the group what got you into this place?"

I stutter over my words. "My parents signed me up."

"You're lying," Cassie sings.

"No, I'm not."

"I'm guessing that you tried to kill yourself," she says.

"I didn't try to kill myself," I say, looking around at the other girls.

"Your boyfriend beats you, but you keep taking him back. Or you're flunking out of school. Am I getting warm?" Cassie mocks.

"No," I say more emphatically. "I have straight As."

"I got it. Maybe . . ." Cassie draws closer and gets into my face. "Maybe you're just a selfish brat who's never experienced anything bad in her life, but Mommy and Daddy caught you screwing your boyfriend on their fine leather couch and couldn't believe their precious child would let a boy put his stick in their innocent child's hole."

My stomach is tight, like a vise is wrapped around my body and is squeezing until everything comes spilling out. I grip on to the wood bench until my nails hurt, but I don't make a sound. I force a yawn in Cassie's face, my neck straining as I suck in air.

"Or maybe it's worse. Maybe you're just an apathetic mess of a human being. A bump waiting to get run over," Cassie scoffs. "And you think I'm crazy. At least I feel things and I'm not afraid to talk about it. Do you even feel anything, Zander?"

Apathetic. In French: *apathique.*

The grief counselor at school, Mrs. Nunez, said the same thing. My dad wanted to send me to what he called a "real professional" at the hospital in Phoenix, but my mom insisted that between her efforts and the school counselor's, I would be fine. She doesn't like hospitals. My dad's compromise was that I would also attend Camp Padua.

"You strike me as very apathetic, Zander," Mrs. Nunez said. "Do you know what apathetic means?"

"I have an A in English." I looked out the window.

"Yes." She shuffled my personal folder around on her desk. "You have As in all your classes. Which is why I'm confused how all of this happened. You're smart, Zander. You should know better."

"It won't happen again," I said.

"I know you must be having a hard time with what happened to your sister, but to go to such extreme lengths . . ." She touched my leg.

"It won't happen again." I said louder.

"Have you cried much since it happened?"

"Sure," I said. A few weeks earlier Coop was tickling me on my bed, which was code for really just trying to get my shirt off. I lay still and stared at the ceiling, conjugating French verbs. I barely felt him touching me.

He sat back all of a sudden and said, "Holy shit. You're crying. That is so fucked up, Zander."

He left and I didn't care.

"I cry all the time," I told Mrs. Nunez.

She seemed satisfied and went a different direction after that.

"I'm good at organizing. Let's plan for your future, since you've told me you intend to have an actual future," she said. I took home a list of potential universities, and my mom put it under one of her inspirational magnets on the fridge that says, "The present is a present."

But right now, this present is no gift. Cassie gets in my face again. "Are you ignoring me, Zander? Focusing on something easier to deal with? Pretending I don't exist? Too bad for you, but I do exist. I'm one hundred percent real, whether you want to see it or not."

"That's enough, Cassie," Madison says.

I shake in my seat in the Circle of Hope as Cassie begins to sit back down. I might break the bench with my bare fingers or use Cassie's fork to poke her own eyes out.

"Maybe you're the liar," I blurt out.

"What?" Cassie turns slowly back toward me.

"You didn't share anything about yourself. How do we know there's even anything *to* share? You could be lying about it all," I say.

"You want me to share something about myself?" When Cassie comes closer to me, her sweet breath hits my nose. She puts her foot up on the bench. "Do you see this?" She points to a large raised scar on her shin that's multiple inches long. I can't believe I haven't noticed it before. But then again, I haven't noticed a lot of things lately. "This is from being thrown down the stairs by my mom's boyfriend. He thought it was fun to beat the shit out of a five-year-old while my mom watched. Have you ever felt a rusty nail tear your skin, *Zander*?"

Blood drains from my face, but no words manage to come out of my mouth.

"I'm sorry that happened to you," Madison finally says.

"Are you really sorry, Mads? Or are you just sorry that you have to deal with me?" Cassie tosses the St. Anthony figurine into the dirt at my feet. "I'm done here."

She walks away from the Circle of Hope. I dig my foot back into the ground and press as hard as I can, pushing the dirt until the raging anger in my stomach goes away. I wish it would all just go away.

"I think that's enough for today," Madison says, picking up St. Anthony and putting him back in her pocket.

CHAPTER 7

Dear Mom and President Cleveland,

I've met a girl. And she's real. I'll keep you posted.

Your son,

Grover Cleveland

Cassie doesn't come to dinner. I make a spinach salad, but I'm not very hungry. My stomach feels like someone punched me. It hurts all over. I stop in front of a tray of cookies the size of my head, most definitely not homemade. They look like something mass-produced with an expiration date of never.

Eating mass-produced food is equivalent to eating raw pesticides, my mom always says.

I set a cookie on my tray and take a seat next to Grover.

"Where's Sticks?" he asks.

"I don't know," I say flatly. I poke at my salad, popping a cherry tomato into my mouth. It tastes like acid going down my throat.

"She ran away," Bek says.

"She did?" I practically yell.

"With my heart." Bek smiles, but Grover doesn't say anything. Every few seconds Grover glances over at me.

"What?" I ask.

"Nothing." Grover shrugs.

I eat, trying to ignore the rotten feeling inside of me. It's what my parents don't understand. Feeling good only makes feeling bad worse. Way worse. I just want to be even. There's nothing wrong with that. But it's impossible right now. Cassie pushed on me so hard I can't ignore the anger I feel, but at the same time, I'm sad for her. And what I want to feel is indifferent. Caring causes pain, no matter how much or little you care.

When I can't stand another bite of the garden on my plate, I unwrap the cookie. Then I rewrap it. Then I unwrap it. Then I lick the sweet crumbs from my fingers. I look around the mess hall wondering if anyone noticed, but no one is paying attention, except Grover. He just sits next to me occasionally touching his bare knee to mine under the table. Every time it happens I scoot over, but somehow he always finds a way to do it again.

At the end of dinner, he sets an apple down on my tray.

"In case you change your mind," he says. But I hand it back to him. "You know some people like to peel off the skin because it makes it easier to eat."

"So?" I ask.

"So even if you peel off the skin, the poison's still inside."

"I'm still not eating it," I say.

"Who said anything about eating it? I just want you to understand it." Grover touches Cassie's empty seat. "Under a hard exterior there's usually something sweet."

I get his more-than-obvious hint. "But what about the poison in the seeds?"

"Every apple has poison inside. If we're careful enough, we can cut out the seeds. But it takes patience."

"I thought you said you hate waiting," I say.

"I do hate waiting." Grover smiles at me. "But it sure beats poison."

"So what's your poison?" I ask, crossing my arms over my chest.

Grover takes the apple and tosses it in the air. He catches it easily. "Maybe tomorrow," he says.

Cassie is in the cabin when we get back. She smells like Lemonheads. No one says anything and she says nothing back. She just reaches into her duffel bag and pulls out a red container of nail polish. She sits on top of her bed, painting her toenails and every few minutes popping another Lemonhead in her mouth.

As I lie across from her, I can't help but look at the scar on her leg. How did I not notice it before?

"If you keep looking at me, Z, I'm going to nail polish your forehead in the middle of the night."

When I wake up somewhere between twilight and morning, Cassie's bed sits empty and, in the bathroom, the window is pushed open. I stand up on the toilet seat and try to close it, but I can't.

Instead, I push the window open farther, so Cassie doesn't have a hard time climbing back in.

CHAPTER 8

Aunt Chey,

It's about time I tell you that I had sex in your bed . . . with your boyfriend.

Kisses,

Cassie

I try volleyball, arts and crafts, and horseback riding. I even play Bek in tetherball one afternoon after another torturous group "share-apy" session. In an exercise to get to know ourselves better, Madison asks the group to share one thing about themselves they've never told anyone. Katie says she cheated on a math test her freshman year. Hannah says she kissed her best friend's boyfriend. Dori says that most days she's pretty sure there's no God, which would really piss off her Bible-thumping stepdad. I say I hate spinach.

"Then why do you eat a fucking spinach salad every night?" Cassie counters me.

I look down at my feet and try to remember the word for *spinach* in French, but come up blank.

"What about you, Cassie? What have you never told anyone?" Madison asks.

Cassie clicks her tongue on the roof of her mouth. "I've never told anyone that it's weird that Zander eats spinach when she hates it."

After that, I head straight to the tetherball courts. I like the feeling of punching something, but it catches me off guard—the sensation of actually liking something and wanting to do it again. I can't remember the last time that happened. To my surprise, I end up winning. Hayes cheers from the sidelines chanting, "Durga! Durga! Durga!" Bek doesn't look too disappointed and claims his artificial arm holds him back.

"Why do you lie all the time?" I ask.

"I don't." He rubs his very apparent arm and walks away.

An afternoon later that week, I lie alone on the raft, air-drying myself after a swim. It's another thing I'd forgotten—how much I like being in the water. Or maybe I didn't forget; I just didn't care to remember. Out in the middle of the lake, it almost feels like I'm not at camp. My eyes glaze over and my mind fades away, but I realize that if I'm not at camp that means I'm at home and the anger comes back. I squeeze my nails into my palms. As I feared, the downside to actually acknowledging that I like something is that I notice when I *don't* like something, too.

The raft starts to move as Grover climbs up the ladder and shakes his wet hair over me. Little droplets of water fall on my face.

"Finally, the legendary black bathing suit. All my dreams have come true." He sets an apple next to me. "You didn't take this at lunch."

"How many times do I have to tell you, I don't want it?" I roll over onto my side.

"A boy can try." He tosses the whole apple into the water. It splashes through the surface, but comes back up seconds later and floats.

"You're just gonna waste it?" I ask.

"You know the whole 'eat an apple a day to keep the doctor away' thing doesn't really apply to me." Grover watches the ripples on the water.

"How do you *know* you're going to be schizophrenic?"

"I don't know. But I feel it."

Feel. I nod at the word.

"What's it like?" I ask.

"Like sitting on a wobbly chair that will eventually break from the pressure." Grover looks at the bobbling apple for a second before coming back to me. "But let's not talk about me. Let's talk about you."

"No." I lie back down and turn my face up to the sun. A second later, I feel a shadow block the heat. I open my eyes and see Grover's face inches from mine.

"You're really pretty. Does your boyfriend who plays football tell you that?"

I don't move. I just look into Grover's oversized eyes.

"He should," he says.

"He doesn't really care about me," I say. "He just likes my boobs."

"I can't blame him for that." Grover smiles. "How do you know he doesn't care about you?"

My stomach turns with anger. Again. When I try to push the feeling down, I hear Cassie's voice in my ear. *Apathetic mess.* It makes the anger worse and I can't get rid of it.

"Because he always forgets my sister's birthday," I say. I've never said that out loud before.

"You have a sister? What's her name?" Water drips from Grover's hair onto my forehead.

"Molly."

I acknowledge Molly.

"When is Molly's birthday?"

"September sixteenth."

"I'll write it down in my notebook when I get back to the beach. I can send her a card. Do you want to dump your boyfriend yet?"

"You don't have to do that."

"I want to do that," Grover says.

"Well, she won't get it."

"Is she off at college?"

"No, she's younger than me," I say.

"Boarding school? I can send it there."

"She's dead, Grover."

The moment the words come out, my chest feels like a balloon pops inside of me. I deflate. Grover stays still, his eyes barely blinking. "You should definitely dump your boyfriend," he says.

"I acknowledge that." I close my eyes. The strain of looking at Grover so closely that I can see the pores on his nose and the freckles that rim his eyes makes my sight blurry. Nothing is spoken for too many long seconds. I try to find a verb to conjugate in French in my head, but it's a jumbled mess.

"Why do you care so much about Cassie? She's so mean," I finally say.

"How does that make you feel?"

Feel. The word is haunting me.

"Cassie makes me mad," I admit.

"Then it's working." I look at Grover, confused. "If you're mad at her, then she can be mad at you. Get it?" He smiles.

"And being mad is a good thing?"

"What's wrong with being mad?" Grover asks. I can't muster the energy to respond. Being mad means *being*, and some days, I simply don't want to be. "You may not want to be mad, Zander, but maybe you need to be."

"How do you know?"

"I don't. Only you know yourself." Grover leans in closer to me, like he's telling me a secret. "I care because she doesn't want me to," he says.

"But if Cassie doesn't want you to care about her, why not give her what she wants?"

"It's not about doing what people want you to do. It's about giving people what they need." Grover moves in closer, his nose inches from my face. For a moment, I think he's going to kiss me and my heart rate picks up. "I want to remember you like this for the rest of my life."

And then he sits back. The sun hits me directly in the eyes, making them instantly water.

"You should really think about dumping that boyfriend of yours," Grover says.

"What about you?" I sit up. "What makes you mad?"

Grover smiles and does a cannonball into the water, splashing me. Chills cover my skin and when his head pops up, he yells, "I can wait for you, Zander!"

"I thought you said you hate waiting."

"I do." Water drips down Grover's face. "But that doesn't mean I don't need to do it."

He swims away as I sit sweating in the afternoon sun. When I get too hot, I dive off the raft and swim all the way to the bottom of the lake. My hair floats around me as I sit on the floor of Lake Kimball. I grab a fistful of sand and let it drain out of my hand slowly, like grains dripping through an hourglass. I try to clear my brain. When the pinch of suffocation starts in my lungs, I kick my way to the top and gasp for air. A second later and I might not have made it.

On the beach, I find Cassie sitting on her towel. Her nose points up to the sky as she leans back on her hands. I dry off and twist my wet hair into a ponytail. A few strands come loose in my hand. They cling to my damp fingers.

"Damn it," I whisper.

"Talking to yourself again, Z?"

I wipe the strands on my towel and let them go.

"I pull on my hair too hard when I'm frustrated. I'm afraid I might go bald," I admit. "I also have a sister."

"Like I care," Cassie says.

"And she's dead." Cassie looks at me, but I can't read her face. "I haven't said that out loud much." I stretch my hands out at my side and resist the urge to clench up. "I can teach you how to swim," I say.

Cassie's face turns sour. "Who said I don't know how to swim?"

"No one. I just guessed."

Cassie blows out an exaggerated breath. "Who even says I want to know how to swim? If it means I have to wear a bathing suit like yours, I'd rather drown."

"Fine," I say and kick some sand on her towel. "But if you decide you need me, you know where to find me."

TEAMWORK

CHAPTER 9

Mom and Dad,
Thanks for the bug spray.
Z

After a week of camp, Dori decides to drop the bomb in group share-apy that she tried to kill herself once.

"It was a few years ago, right after my mom got remarried. I locked myself in the bathroom and ate a bottle of pills. I just grabbed the first thing I could find and downed it," she says.

"Oh my God," Hannah speaks up.

"It wasn't that bad." Dori shakes her head. "I was crying so hard I couldn't see the label on the bottle. Turns out I downed a bottle of Beano. Nothing even happened."

Cassie bursts out laughing. "Well, your first mistake was taking pills. What a sissy fucking suicide."

Dori ignores her. "In the end, it was a good thing. I realized I didn't really want to die. I was just being dramatic."

"Dori, that's so scary," Madison says. "What if you had really hurt yourself?"

"You don't think I registered that?" Dori snaps. "I would have left my mom alone to live with her Neanderthal husband." She rolls her eyes at Madison, but Madison doesn't seem to let it get to her.

She touches Dori's leg and says, "Thank you for sharing." Madison turns to the rest of the group. "Has anyone else ever thought about going to dramatic lengths with their lives?"

"That's a stupid question, Mads. Of course we have. We're here."

"I've never tried to kill myself," Hannah says.

"No. You just mutilate your body. I'd say that's dramatic, Razor Blades."

"I don't cut myself with razor blades."

"You want to judge Dori because she tried to off herself with Beano, but you're just as bad as she is," Cassie scoffs.

After that, the rest of the session goes flat.

The next day, I sit on the end of my bed, my foot tapping on the ground in an even rhythm. It always helps if I keep a beat.

"*Devenir, Revenir, Monter, Rester, Sortir,*" I whisper to myself, my toes slowly becoming numb. "*Venir, Aller, Naître, Descendre, Entrer, Rentrer* . . ." I stop blank. My foot hangs above the ground ready to pound out the next beat, but the word isn't there. "Dr. and Mrs. Vandertramp" verbs are my French mnemonic device specialty. I know them like I know the smell of my own house.

I run my hands through my hair, but the moment before I pull a few strands free, I pause. My fingers feel around my scalp, inspecting the density. I would have more hair if I could just stop pulling on myself so hard. It doesn't help me. It hurts me. I drop my hands, rest my head in my palms, and look around the cabin like the French verb I can't seem to find in my brain is hiding somewhere in here.

"What the hell comes next?" I whisper.

Dori enters the cabin a bit later with a stack of letters in her hands. She holds one out to me.

"Mail delivery. Also, Madison said to meet in the Circle of Hope in fifteen minutes."

"Thanks." I take the letter and recognize the handwriting and return address. *Nina Osborne.*

"Aren't you gonna open it?" Dori asks.

"It's from my mom."

She waves one of her letters in the air. "I get it. My mom just told me she's pregnant. In a letter. Which means she's having sex with my disgusting stepdad. I want to puke." Dori plops down on the bed next to me. "I can't believe some of my genes are going to mix with his and create a person. I hate him."

Some afternoons Dori will say she's going to an activity, but I'll find her sleeping in the cabin. I never wake her up.

"I'm sorry your mom is having a baby with someone you hate," I say.

"That's okay." The skin around her mouth hangs low, like it's heavy.

When Dori is about to leave the cabin, I blurt out, "How do you know you're depressed?"

Dori stops and touches the lock on the door, circling her finger around the metal. "Because some days I don't think there's any point to this."

"To camp?" I ask.

"No, Zander. To life."

Dori quietly shuts the door and leaves. I flip the flimsy letter around in my hand a few times. I contemplate burning it, but with the humidity from all the rain, I don't think it would light.

So I open it instead.

Dear Zander,

It sure is quiet around here without you. Your father formed a "podcast club." I'm not sure you could call it a club since the only two members are he and I, but I don't tell him that. He makes me listen to TED Talks and Freakonomics Radio and a whole bunch of other stuff that you would find horribly boring. It's not as bad as I thought, though. I think I'm actually learning something.

That's what I've decided this summer is all about. Learning. You're learning in Michigan and your father and I are learning here at home. I'm not sure I'll ever learn to get used to the silence of not having you around, though. I still wish the camp had made an exception on the "no cell phone" rule for you. We've been through so much, it just seems cruel to keep me away from my daughter.

Anyway, I hope you're enjoying yourself. I can't tell by your letters. They're so short.

I saw Cooper working at the grocery store last week. He looked too busy to come say hi, but I waved. I hope they're feeding you well at camp. I just listened to a podcast about the overabundance of sugar in our food. Yellow foods in particular. Stay away from yellow. And orange. Nothing is naturally orange unless it's an actual orange or a carrot. You can eat those.

I miss you.

Love,

Mom

I stare down at her pointed handwriting, like the words have thorns on the end. Each mundane sentence pricks me. I ball up the letter and I grab a piece of paper and a pen from my duffel bag.

I write:

Devenir

Revenir

Monter
Rester
Sortir
Venir
Aller
Naître
Descendre
Entrer
Rentrer

My foot taps to the beat as I say the words in my head again and again, but every few seconds my eyes drift to the balled-up letter sitting next to me.

When I can't stand it anymore, I throw my mom's letter away and start searching the mound of clothes on Cassie's bed. I know they're here somewhere. I shake a pair of shorts and hear something rattle—Lemonheads. I pop three in my mouth like pills. Sweet, sugary, *yellow* pills. My cheeks water as I crunch down on the candy. I fold up my unfinished French mnemonic device and put it in an envelope addressed to my mom.

On my way to the Circle of Hope, I detour to the outgoing mailbox by the mess hall and drop the letter in the slot.

"Breaking up with your boyfriend?" Grover says from behind me.

My heart rate jumps in surprise. "No. It's a letter for my mom."

"Did you tell her about me?" he asks.

"No. I told her about me. She won't get it, though."

Grover nods as silence hangs over us. I can't think of what to say because it's never just talking with Grover. His big eyes always look like he's about to cry. It makes every word he utters seem like it's his last, and I want to grab him and make it all go away. And Grover's hair is wet right now. He's wearing soaking-wet swim trunks and a "Having fun isn't hard when you have a library card" T-shirt.

He leans in toward me. "Is that?"

I back away. "What?"

He looks at my lip. "Sugar."

I cup my hand over my mouth and smell my own breath.

"Don't tell Cassie," I say.

Grover smiles and presses his lips together. Neither of us moves.

"I hate the way my mom says things without really saying things," I finally blurt out.

"Like what?"

"She hates the letters I send home, but she won't actually say that. She'll just say they're too short, but what she really means is that they aren't enough. There's a difference." Grover's eyes do the almost-crying thing and my stomach gets tight, like I want to burst open. "It's like she wants everything to be long and drawn out because it's better to have noise than nothing. But you could write a thousand words and it still wouldn't equal the power of 'I love you.'"

"I love you," Grover says.

"Exactly. 'I love you.'"

"You better tell your boyfriend."

"Wait. What? I was making an analogy," I say.

"I think it was more like an acknowledgment." Grover winks.

I groan and start to walk away, shaking my head. Damn his overactive eyes.

"Wait," he says, catching up to me and touching my arm. I yank it away.

"I told you. I hate waiting," I snap.

"And I told you that sometimes waiting is inevitable. So stop fighting it."

"I'm not fighting anything."

"Yes, you are," Grover says.

"No, I'm not." I hold his stare. The watery sheen on his skin makes the sun reflect off of his nose. I notice that the tip of it is perfectly round and smooth. "What about you?" I say.

"What about me?"

"You never acknowledge anything."

"Yes, I do. In fact, I'd like to acknowledge right now that you smell good. Sugar suits you."

"That doesn't count."

"Sure it does."

"But it's not about *you*," I say.

"People are too selfish. Did you know that if given a choice more people would rather win the lottery than cure AIDS?"

"Forget it." I start to walk away.

"You're just as bad as your mom," Grover hollers after me.

I whip around. "How can you say that?"

He makes up the space between us. "You say she likes to drag things out. So do you."

"No, I don't." I move again, but Grover moves with me.

"Yes, you do. You're doing it right now."

I take another step back and I run into a tree. My head knocks against the bark with a small thud and I'm pinned.

"Is your head okay?" he asks.

"Obviously not. I'm here, aren't I?"

"I meant this head." Grover touches the tender spot on the back of my skull. And then he backs away from me, so far that the air gets cold, like when the sun goes down in the desert. "I'm sure your mom will appreciate the letter no matter what. She's probably been waiting for it."

He walks away and I slump down on the tree, pulling my knees to my chest to bury my face. My eyes get tired as I sit on the ground, my energy waning. I contemplate pulling a Dori move and skipping group share-apy to take a nap. But the more I think about Coop, the more the fatigue fades and anger replaces it. I want to call him and scream at him for not talking to my mom at the grocery store. My mom may not like to see reality, but even she must know he wasn't too busy to talk to her. Coop avoided her.

On my way over to the Circle of Hope, I pass the tetherball court. Without hesitating, I smack the ball with as much force as I can, sending it high into the air. The ball wraps around the pole quickly, making a ding sound when all the slack in the rope is gone. I smack it again with the other hand.

"Durga, Durga, Durga," I say through tight teeth. It's clear my tetherball skills have greatly improved, though this place hasn't stopped me from talking to myself.

CHAPTER 10

Aunt Chey,

Don't look under my bed.

Kisses,

Cassie

"When I say the word *teamwork*, what comes to your mind first?" Madison asks.

"An over-Botoxed face," Cassie says. She's braiding small patches of random hair on her head. They stick out chaotically like broken antennas. I count seven braids total. Cassie stops midbraid. "Sorry. I should have been more specific. *Your* over-Botoxed face."

"I don't Botox my face."

"Not now, but you will." She goes back to work on her hair. "I can picture it. In twenty years, you'll be one of those women with a shiny flat forehead and plastic cheekbones, whose upper lip doesn't move. I bet you go running to the dermatologist on your twenty-fifth birthday when you see your first wrinkle."

"I meant the question seriously, Cassie."

"I wasn't trying to be funny, Mads," Cassie says deadpan, tying a rubber band around the end of a braid. "I was trying to be *honest*. When you say anything, your future plastic face comes to my mind first."

"Well, I'd thank you for your honesty, but I don't appreciate it."

"Most people don't," Cassie says, leaning back on her hands and turning her face up to the sky. "When you're wrinkled from too many sunburns from too many spring breaks in Panama City, where you've screwed some guy with an eagle tattoo who looked cute through your beer goggles, you'll be jealous of my skin. I'll be eighty before I wrinkle." Cassie sits back and smiles. "If I choose to live that long."

For the first time since camp started, Madison looks defeated. The girl with the perfect nails and long silky hair, who appears unbreakable, might be on the verge of cracking.

"There's no *I* in team," I blurt out, wanting the moment to be over between Cassie and Madison. Everyone turns to look at me. "You wanted to know what I think about when you say *teamwork*? 'There's no *I* in team.' That's what my coach always said."

"Your swim coach?" Madison asks, her shoulders relaxing.

I nod. "I pointed out once that there *is* a *me*, if you rearrange the letters. He ignored me."

Madison hands me the St. Anthony statue and whispers, "Thank you."

I roll the little man around in my hands. I haven't talked much in group share-apy before today.

"Tell us more about swim team," Madison says.

"My coach smelled like garlic. Have you ever been in a humid enclosed space with someone who smells like garlic?" I ask the question down at St. Anthony as if I'm talking to him. "It's like every molecule of air is carrying the world's worst case of bad breath."

"That is *so* gross," Dori says.

"I tried breathing through my mouth once, thinking I wouldn't smell the garlic, but then it was like I was tasting it," I say.

"Oh my God, Z, I'm gonna throw up." Cassie sticks her finger down her throat and looks at Katie. "Fingers, care to join me?"

"Shut up." Katie glares at Cassie.

"'Teamwork makes the dream work,'" I continue. "That's the other thing he used to say."

"My volleyball coach used to say that." Madison smiles. "Coaches must get a manual with these sayings inside."

"Kind of like camp counselors," Cassie snaps at her.

But I ignore their banter. I clutch the St. Anthony figurine, slowly trying to suffocate the plastic man in my tight hand. "He said it before every meet. And I would stand there, trying not to breathe in whatever he ate for dinner the night before, thinking *what dream is he talking about?* The dream of winning our relay? The whole damn swim meet? Those aren't dreams. Those are accomplishments. And stupid ones at that."

"Well, did you win?" Dori asks.

"Every time," I say and then correct myself. "Almost every time."

"Winning isn't a stupid accomplishment, Zander. It feels good. You should be proud of the fact that you're a good swimmer," Madison says.

"That's my point. It didn't feel good," I say.

"Well, then how *did* it feel?" she asks.

I set the St. Anthony figurine down next to me on the bench.

"It didn't feel like anything." I make it a point to glance at Cassie before I finally say, "*I* didn't feel anything."

The circle goes quiet for a while. When I can't stand the silence in my head, I repeat the Camp Padua prayer over and over since I can't remember my French words. Anything is better than silence.

We pray to Saint Anthony that the lost be found. That the soul be free. That life be everlasting.

Over and over. Over and over. Blocking out the dead air.

Madison eventually moves on and says we're going to play a team-building game. We're all on a plane and it's going down, but there's a boat that will save us and get us to a deserted island. We can take one thing as a group, but we all have to agree.

"You have five minutes to decide. Now is the time to work together, ladies." Madison looks down at her watch before telling us to start.

It takes a while for anyone to pipe up, but eventually Cassie does. "We don't need five minutes because I know what we need."

"We need water," Katie says.

"No we don't, Fingers. We're surrounded by water."

"You can't drink salt water," Katie counters.

"We'll boil it." Cassie shrugs.

"Then we need matches," Dori says.

"That's a waste. We can just rub two sticks together," Cassie says.

Madison taps her foot on the ground. "Three minutes."

"What about a phone?" Hannah offers.

"Yes, I'm sure Verizon has a cell tower on a deserted island, Razor Blades. Genius." Cassie shakes her head.

"Don't call me Razor Blades."

"Why not? You're cutting up your limbs for attention. I'm just paying attention."

"I don't cut myself for attention."

"Then why do you cut yourself?" Cassie crosses her arms and gives Hannah a look of real curiosity.

Hannah looks around at the group. "I still think a phone is a good idea."

"Thirty seconds," Madison sings.

"It's a terrible idea and I already told you I know what we need."

"So tell us," I say.

Cassie gets a crooked smile on her face and talks slowly. "If I was on a plane that was going down . . ."

"Fifteen seconds," Madison says.

"And the only option was living on a deserted island with the four of you . . ." Cassie leans in and talks in a hushed voice. ". . . I'd grab a bottle of Beano, so I can kill myself."

"Time's up." Madison says with an exhale. "You're all dead."

Cassie smiles. "Guess I won't need the Beano after all."

CHAPTER 11

Mom,

Podcast club sounds horrible.

Z

PS—Sorry about the letter.

The rain starts just before dinner. A crack of thunder ripples through the sky right as I make it to the mess hall. I hold my arm out and let a few drops of rain hit my skin. The bonfire Kerry promised us tonight will most likely be cancelled. I won't complain about that. I got twenty new mosquito bites a few nights ago while we sat around the Circle of Hope with Hayes leading us in singing old cowboy songs and "Kumbaya" as he played the guitar.

A raindrop sits on my arm on top of one of my swollen bites. I rub the water into my skin. I'm glad it's raining.

Bek sits alone at our dinner table before anybody else makes it to the mess hall. I grab a salad and lemonade, and then I go back and add a dollop of yellow-and-orange macaroni and cheese to my plate.

"I need your help," I say to Bek as I sit down.

He takes a bite out of his fried chicken. "Who are you?"

"Zander."

"I don't know a Zander."

"Cut it out, Bek. I'm having a problem remembering my French words." I pick at my macaroni. It's definitely the kind made with powdered cheese.

"Who's Bek?"

"You," I say.

"I don't know a Bek."

"Fine. Alex, I need your help. You're the only person here who speaks French."

"I thought you said my name is Bek."

"It is."

"Then who is this Alex you speak of?" he asks.

"That's you, too."

"I believe you have mistaken me for an old French boyfriend of yours named Alex Bek. Though I will say, that doesn't sound like a French name. What's your name again?" Bek asks.

"We've been sitting at the same table for over a week, Bek. My name is Zander." Right then, Grover sits down next to me with his tray full of food. My stomach goes from being properly placed in my belly to clogging my throat. I glance at him out of the corner of my eye.

"Welcome to our table," Bek says to Grover. "You wouldn't happen to be Alex Bek? Zander, here, is looking for her ex-French boyfriend."

"The name's Grover Cleveland." He holds out his hand. "I'm Zander's future boyfriend."

All my body heat travels to my face and I want to punch Grover, and at the same time, I don't. I couldn't hurt him. I just don't know *what* I want from him.

"It's nice to meet you, future boyfriend of Zander, Grover Cleveland." Bek shakes his hand like this is the first time they've ever met.

"Same here." He nods.

"What is going on?" I ask.

"I don't know," Bek says.

"Of course, you don't." Grover pats him on the back. "You were hit in the head by a baseball and now are suffering traumatic amnesia from the collision."

"How do you know?" Bek asks Grover.

"I saw it happen."

I groan. "You both are ridiculous." I shovel a large spoonful of macaroni into my mouth.

"I acknowledge that." Grover winks at me.

"I don't," Bek says.

I should have known better than to ask Bek for help. We don't even know if Alex Trebek is his real name. But my frustration begins to melt as the rich, buttery taste of macaroni and cheese coats my mouth. The film stays on my teeth and tongue.

"Oh my God," I moan.

"You can just call me Grover."

I ignore the comment and shovel another spoonful into my mouth and another.

"Take it easy there, Little Miss Piggy." Cassie plops down in her seat with a tray full of cherry tomatoes and cucumbers.

"Shut up," I say with a full my mouth. "It's so good."

"It's macaroni and cheese, Z, not an orgasm." Cassie bites down on a cucumber.

"You've had an orgasm?" Bek asks. "Tell me about it."

"You wish, Baby Fat."

"I thought my name is Bek."

"It is." Grover pats Bek on the back again and he asks me, "Haven't you ever had macaroni and cheese?"

I stop midchew. The entire table turns to look at me. I swallow the food in my mouth with a gulp.

"Sure." I wipe my lips clean.

"You're lying," Bek taunts and points at my face.

"You should know," I bite back.

"Macaroni and cheese is like a fucking kid food group. Everybody eats macaroni and cheese. What the hell is wrong with your family, Z?" Cassie asks.

I flinch at Cassie's words. What *is* wrong with my family? How do I tell her nothing and everything at the same time?

"Seriously, you've never had mac and cheese?" Grover asks, leaning on the table, his eyes searching mine. I silently beg him not to blink, for fear a tear would run down his cheek and I'd have to wipe his skin dry and admit that I can't remember the last time I saw powdered cheese.

Kerry claps three times to get everyone's attention. "The only way to be found," he yells. I blink and look away. I set my spoon down and push my tray away from me.

Is to admit we're lost . . .

"Due to the rain, we have to change our plans for this evening. Instead, tonight will be game night." Kerry points to a large cabinet filled with board games sitting in the corner of the room. "When you've cleaned up your dinner, feel free to grab a game and let the fun begin. Those needing nightly medication can see the nurse at the Wellness Center."

The macaroni and cheese on my tray stays untouched for the rest of dinner. When I'm done, I dump it into the trash.

Solitaire. That's what I want to play tonight. I attempt to grab a deck of cards from the game cabinet when Grover steps in my way.

"*Guess who?*"

"Is this another one of your games with Bek?" I ask and try to move around him, but he steps in my way.

"No."

"Then what is it?" I ask.

"*Guess who?*"

"I don't need to guess who!" I yell. "I know who you are. You're Grover Cleveland."

"No," he says with a crooked smile on his face, and then he holds up a box. "Guess Who? The game. Do you want to play with me?"

I look around at the people staring at me. And they *are* staring.

"Fine." I snatch the box from Grover's hands.

"By the way, you're cute when you're mad."

"I'm not mad. I'm frustrated." I set the game down on the table and open the box.

"That's good."

"How is that good?" I ask.

"Do you know how many people in this world don't actually *know* how they feel? I mean, with my heightened emotional state, I have a hard time identifying ham from turkey on my sandwiches, let alone how I feel. And actually both sound really good right now."

"You should try it," I say.

"What? Ham or turkey?"

"No. Admitting to how you feel."

"You know how I feel." Grover wiggles his eyebrows at me.

"About me, maybe. But not about you."

"Well, I guess right now I feel hungry," he says.

"We just ate."

"You know what sounds good? Saltines. Did you know that it's virtually impossible to eat six saltines in under a minute?"

"What?" I ask, confused as to how we got to this topic.

"Yeah, your mouth gets too dry." Grover nods. "We should try it." He's gone from his seat before I can tell him that I'm not hungry for saltines or any other food. I should have stuck with the solitaire, but Grover always seems to trap me. He won't take no for an answer, and part of me likes it, but the other part desperately just wants him to leave me alone.

"Found them." Grover plops back down in his seat. He pulls a bunch of individually wrapped saltine crackers, like the kind restaurants give out with soup, from his pockets. He leans over the table to hide the stash with his arms.

"Where did you find those?" I ask.

"In the kitchen."

"How'd you get in the kitchen?"

"Not telling." Grover smiles. "Now, who goes first?"

"I'm not doing this."

"Come on. Don't you want to see if you can do it?" he asks.

"Who cares if I can eat six saltines in under sixty seconds?"

"I care."

"Why?" I lean in and rest my arms on the table, mimicking his posture.

"Because it will prove my point."

"And what point is that?" I ask.

"That you're not like anyone else in the whole world. That the odds of there ever being another person exactly like you is one in infinity." Grover lays his hand on top of mine and his face turns serious. "And before I go crazy, I want to be able to brag that I know a *real* person who can eat six saltines in under sixty seconds."

I glance down at his hand that's over mine. Not one speck of my skin is showing. He's covering me.

"Fine." I grab the crackers and start unwrapping them.

"The rule is one minute, no water, and you have to eat every crumb," Grover says, glancing at the clock.

"I can't believe I'm doing this."

"I can." Grover winks at me. "Are you ready?" When I nod, he takes one more look around and whispers, "Go!"

I start to shovel in crackers. They're salty and taste delicious. I swallow a few bites before the saltines start to congeal in my cheeks. I work them around with my tongue, gulping down small pieces.

"You're cute when you binge."

"Shut up," I hiss with a cracker lisp and spit a few crumbs on the table.

Grover points. "You have to eat those."

"Shut up!" I pick them off the table and pop them in my mouth. I can't believe I'm eating already-been-chewed bits of food off a dirty mess-hall table. I'm sure my parents didn't read about this in the camp brochure.

"Thirty seconds."

Grover's eyes focus on me like this is the greatest thing he's ever seen. I smack my lips together, trying to find any sort of saliva that might help get the crackers down my throat. I don't want to let him down. He finally admitted something about himself, a thing I've noticed he never does. And I want to do this for him. I need to. As I chew, I realize at this moment I wish I could fix the proverbial broken chair Grover is sitting on. I wish I could hold it together so his life never falls apart.

"Ten seconds," he says.

But the dryness sets in. I swallow a little chunk and then another one, but it's not happening fast enough. My mouth is a desert.

"Five seconds."

I make one last attempt to take down everything in my mouth, but nothing happens. You can't prevent life from falling apart. That's what it does best. It crumbles and withers and wilts until nothing but crumbs and lost pieces are left. When time is up, I sit across from Grover, my mouth full of saltines.

"That was awesome," he says.

I swallow until my mouth is empty. "See. I'm just like everyone else."

"With saltines, maybe." Grover wipes a crumb from the table. He holds out the game cards to Guess Who? And just like that, we move on, like I didn't just let him down. "You start," he says.

I glance down at the person I've pulled. His name is George. He has blond hair and glasses and resembles my dad slightly.

"Does your person have red hair?" I ask.

Grover shakes his head. "No."

I flip down all the people on my board with red hair.

"Does *your* person have red hair?"

"No."

Grover knocks down his people.

"Does your person have blue eyes?"

"Yes." Grover blinks repeatedly.

I knock down everyone with brown or green eyes until I have seven people left.

"Does your person have glasses?" Grover asks.

"Yes," I groan.

Grover knocks down his entire board so that only three people are left.

"Does your person have a hat on?" I ask.

"No."

I knock down one person.

"Did you play this game when you were little?" he asks.

"Why?"

"Just asking."

"Yes," I say. "Does your person have brown hair?"

"Did you play with Molly?"

"Does your person have brown hair?" I repeat.

"It's my turn to ask the question," Grover says. "Did you play this game with Molly?"

"No." My teeth clench.

"Why not?" he asks.

"She was too little to play. Does your person have brown hair?"

"Still my question. What was Molly like?"

"She had blonde hair," I offer.

"And . . ."

"Brown eyes."

"And . . ."

I groan. "Tan skin. From my mother's side."

Grover flips down all the people on his game board and grabs my hand across the table. "I don't want to know what she looked like, Zander. I want to know who she was."

Grover's hold is strong on me, but it doesn't hurt, more the opposite. His hand is warm, like a blanket. It makes my eyes sting.

"You don't talk about your family," I counter.

"I find you more interesting," he says.

"I think you're avoiding your problems."

"That's true. So are you. We're a perfect pair." Grover rubs his thumb against my skin. "What was Molly like?"

"Let go of my hand."

"No."

"Why do you always have to touch me?"

"Because it reminds me that you're real. And that makes me happy. See, I do admit to some things."

"This doesn't make *me* happy."

"We can't always be happy, Zander," Grover says.

"I know that."

"How do you know that? Is it because of what happened to Molly?"

A bead of sweat drips down my back. I can feel the sweat collecting in my hair. It's not going to stop. This will never stop. The chair will always break and things will fall apart and I will be left with the rotten pieces of what used to be sitting at my feet. And there is no way to put it back together.

I pull my hand free and run from the table, knocking our game all over the floor. Outside, the rain pummels the ground, making everything sloppy. A clap of thunder rolls across the sky, and I jump as I run toward my cabin. But something catches my foot—a rock or tree branch—and I fall. My knee tears open.

"Wait, Zander! Please stop," Grover yells at me.

I whirl around, the weight of anger and sadness and everything else Grover makes me feel when he touches me crushing my chest. I don't want to feel any of it. I want to disappear again. I want to go back to the way I was, when things didn't hurt and I didn't care about the broken pieces at my feet. I run full speed at Grover and hit him in the chest. I hit him as hard as I hit the tetherball. It hurts my hands down to the bone.

"I don't know what Molly was like, okay! I don't know anything about her! Is that what you want to hear?" I yell as I stumble back, my feet unable to keep up with the momentum of my body. The rain falls heavy around us in the darkness. My foot catches something on the ground and twists in an unnatural way as pain shoots up my leg. I yelp as I land in a puddle.

Grover lunges toward me, but I move away from him. My clothes are covered in mud, my hands dirty as I wipe my wet face.

"Don't," I say, my throat burning from holding back tears. I grab my throbbing ankle. "Don't touch me."

I get to my feet, most of my weight resting on my good foot.

"Please, let me take you to the nurse. You're bleeding." Grover points to the stream of blood running down my leg from a gash in my knee.

I turn away from him without saying a word and limp toward the cabin. The pain gets worse with every step I take. Once inside, I get my suitcase out from under my bed and pull out Molly's old quilt. Mud drips on the ground. My sock is soaked with blood from my knee. I want to punch a hole right through the fabric. Instead, I squeeze it with everything I have in me. Then I fall to my knees on the hard cabin floor and stuff my face into the worn fabric. With every inhale, I try to smell her. To smell my little sister like she slept wrapped in this quilt yesterday, but the truth is that she never slept in this quilt—not how I wanted her to sleep in it.

When I finally get up, my leg is crusted over with dry blood. I take off my wet clothes and get in the shower. My ankle is swollen and bruised, but not as bad as I thought it would be. When I'm finished in the bathroom, I hear the rest of the girls and Madison come back to the cabin. I change into my pajama pants and University of Arizona sweatshirt and limp out, ready to climb into bed.

"What the hell happened to you?" Cassie asks as I stuff my wet, bloodied clothes into my laundry bag.

"Nothing."

"Zander, I want you to have freedom this summer, but please don't leave group activities without telling me," Madison says as she locks the door. "I was worried."

"Fine," I say as I climb under Molly's quilt and pull it up to my ears. Mud and blood stain the fabric, but somehow it makes me feel better. Like finally someone actually lived while sleeping with it.

CHAPTER 12

Mom and President Cleveland,

I've decided I want to be a lighthouse operator. Is that what you call a person who guides ships safely into their harbor? Anyway, I'd like to be the guardian of ships.

Please send word if that job still exists. And also more underwear.

Your son,

Grover Cleveland

The window in the bathroom is open, and Cassie's bed is empty when I wake up in the middle of the night. I can feel my heartbeat in my ankle, and my knee throbs like little grains of dirt are slowly manifesting into a bacterial infection. My mom is going to flip if I come back damaged from camp.

I limp to the bathroom and dab my skin with a wet washcloth. At first it stings, but then relief hits. I lean on the sink and stare at the open window. A visceral part of me needs to know just what Cassie does every night by herself.

I climb onto the toilet seat and pull myself up to see how she gets in and out of here. Even with the significant size difference between Cassie and me, I think I can fit through the window easily.

Before I can think about the consequences or how I'll get back in, I fall through the window, landing on the ground on my one foot like a pelican. My flip-flop sinks into the mud a bit as I set my other foot down gingerly. It's exhilarating and liberating. I have to hold in a yelp of excitement. I did it. I escaped a locked room.

The clouds have cleared, and the moon hangs like a crescent just off to the side in the sky. I tiptoe with a limp away from the cabin.

Down at the lake, the dock glows in the moonlight. That's where I find her. Cassie sits staring out at the water. I don't know why I thought she would be here. But she is. I also don't know why I crawled out a small bathroom window with a busted ankle and no way of getting back in. But I did. And it feels good.

The moment I step on the metal dock and it rattles, Cassie jerks to attention.

"What the fuck are you doing here?"

"What the fuck are *you* doing here?" I ask.

"None of your business," Cassie bites. "Don't come any closer."

"Why?"

"I'm afraid your massive body weight is going to sink the dock."

"I don't have massive body weight."

"I saw you put down that macaroni and cheese tonight, fatty." Cassie puffs out her cheeks.

I step closer, ignoring her jabs. Cassie goes rigid, the whites of her eyes becoming more pronounced. "Relax. If the dock sinks, I'll save you, okay?"

"Why would you save me? I wouldn't save you."

"Because at least you're honest about it."

Cassie has a doubtful look on her face. It's odd to see her falter. If she wasn't confident about something, I'm sure she'd be confident about being not confident.

"I promise I'll save you," I say again, and Cassie eases the dagger eyes back a few notches. Her legs hang over the end of the dock, but she keeps her feet flexed so they don't touch the water, like she's hovering above something that might burn her.

"Why are you fucking limping?" she asks as I sit down next to her.

"I twisted my ankle." I pull off my flip-flops and dip my toes into the cold water. I shimmy closer to the edge of the dock so I can immerse my swollen ankle, and I sigh.

"Are you trying to rub it in?" Cassie asks.

"No. This feels good."

Cassie looks off toward the moon, a sharp, annoyed expression on her face.

"I told you, I can teach you how to swim." Her feet stay just inches above the water, as a cooler breeze blows. I wait for her to say something back, but she doesn't. "Aren't you cold?" I ask.

"No."

She's lying. With her lack of body weight, I'd guess she's cold all the time. I pull off my University of Arizona sweatshirt and hand it to her. "Here," I say.

"I said I'm not cold."

"Well, in case you get cold, then." Cassie groans like I just asked her to wear a chicken suit and stand on a street corner dancing with a sign. But it doesn't stop me from handing over the sweatshirt. I know what she needs, even if she doesn't want to admit it.

The reflection of the moon on the surface of the lake makes it look like one big black satin sheet, something slick and smooth. Something someone could disappear under.

"My dad got me the sweatshirt," I say.

"Am I supposed to care?"

"He went to the University of Arizona."

"And I bet you take family trips back there every summer." Cassie's voice gets animated and sarcastically sweet. "Your dad walks you around campus, telling old fraternity stories and claiming those were the best years of his life. And then he buys you a sweatshirt and tells you how he can't wait for you to go there."

I tap the water with my feet, making little ripples. "Actually he ordered the sweatshirt online," I say. Cassie finally looks at me. "Until this summer, the farthest I'd traveled in the past seven years was to a swim meet a few towns over."

"Am I supposed to feel bad for you?"

"No," I say flatly and flick the water again with my toes. "You can have the sweatshirt. I don't want it."

"Like have it forever?" she asks and I nod. Cassie holds it up against her body. "It's way too big for me." But she puts it on.

We sit in silence for a while as I run through a million questions for Cassie that dangle just on the tip of my tongue. Why does she come down here every night? When was the last time someone actually gave her something? Does she remember how much it hurt when she got the scar on her leg? But I don't ask her anything. I hold the questions for later, and for now we just sit together. Sometimes silence is needed the most when life is so full of noise. And Cassie's life must be full of a lot of noise.

At one point Cassie puts her foot so close to the water, I think she's going to touch it, and a moment later, she stands up.

"Wait until I'm off the dock. I don't want you rocking it," she says.

She makes her way toward the beach like she's walking a tightrope, both arms out for balance and right down the center. I wait, watching her, my baggy sweatshirt hanging down almost below her shorts. I slip on my flip-flops and limp over to meet her.

"Tomorrow, you're gonna teach me how to swim," she says. When I nod, Cassie grabs my elbow. Her skin is rough, and I almost pull away out of instinct. She shifts in close, and her arm becomes like a lever holding me up. I take some of the pressure off my bad foot and lean into Cassie as she helps me walk back to the cabin.

At the bathroom window, she groans as she hoists me off the ground.

"No more macaroni and cheese, Z."

"Shut up," I say.

"You shut up."

When I hear the sound of a stick breaking, I stop frozen halfway in the window and look around.

"Did you hear that?" I whisper.

"Relax, Z. What's the worst they can do to us?" Cassie struggles under my weight. "Get in the window. I can't hold you much longer."

I look over my shoulder one more time and spot a long shadow hiding in the trees. It's a familiar shape. Not one I expected to see. And then it disappears.

CHAPTER 13

Cher Papa,

J'ai récemment souffert de paralysie. Je n'ai pas été vacciné contre la poliomyélite. Je réfléchis à ma nouvelle condition.

Cordialement,

Alex Trebek

Puddles of the rain sparkle on the archery field in the morning. It's already hot, and the fact that I have my bathing suit on under my clothes isn't helping. I wipe beads of sweat from my forehead and wave a mosquito off of my skin.

Hayes hands me a plastic bow and arrow set, and I run my hand over the suction cup end. I don't know if Grover will come to archery today, and I haven't decided if I care.

"You're here early," Hayes says.

"I skipped breakfast."

"That's not good, Durga," he says. "If you want to feed your mind, you need to feed your body. Warriors need energy."

"Why do you think I'm a warrior?" I say. I leave out the part in my head that screams that I don't feel like a warrior.

Hayes smiles a slow grin. "We're all warriors in our own internal battles. Durga exists in you *here*." Hayes points at my heart. "But you need food."

He proceeds to tell me about Maslow's hierarchy of needs, which he learned about while getting his childhood development degree. How, if we don't have food and water, we can't feel safe, and if we can't feel safe then we can't feel loved, and if we can't feel loved then we can't have self-esteem, and if we can't feel self-esteem then we can never have full self-actualization.

"All of that stuff starts with food and water?" I ask.

"That's why everyone needs a healthy breakfast, Durga." Hayes pulls a granola bar out of his pocket. "Eat this."

So I do because if Hayes stops calling me Durga, I'll be upset and—realizing that I'll be upset—*feeling* that I'll be upset doesn't bother me so much anymore. If Maslow is right, I'm working my way up the hierarchy, and I don't want to come tumbling down now.

As I eat, someone comes up behind me, and when I turn around, I come face to face with Grover. I practically choke. Maybe I will come tumbling down.

"You weren't at breakfast. Big party last night?" he asks. Grover smiles the type of grin I can't read. Not that I can usually tell what's going to come out of his mouth. Whenever I think I know, I'm reminded I have no idea.

I hold up the granola bar. "Did you know that food is the doorway to self-actualization?"

"And all this time I thought I was eating because of my heightened mental and emotional state."

I don't laugh even though the inside of me wants to. It wants to feel better, which is something so new and different I'm not sure what to do. I press the feeling down with a breath and look at the ground.

"How's your foot?" he asks.

I consciously even out my weight. The pressure pinches my ankle just a little, but soaking it in the cold water last night seems to have helped.

"I'll survive."

"Yes, you will." Grover steps close to me, drawing my attention back up. Part of me wants to punch him in his cute nose and part of me wants to touch his lips so I can feel his smile. Either way, I don't like it. "I brought you something," he says, digging in his pocket.

"You didn't need to . . ." I take a step back from Grover but he grabs me. I cross my arms over my chest as he holds up a bottle.

"Antiseptic. For your knee." He digs deeper. "Neosporin and a Band-Aid. I want you to remember me for the rest of your life but not because I gave you a scar."

"Thanks." I hold out my hand.

"Let me." He kneels down in front of me and touches the tip of his finger to the scab forming on my knee. "It doesn't look too bad."

"Don't." I pull away from his touch.

Grover looks up at me with his big eyes. For the first time, he doesn't look like the confident Grover I've seen every day. He looks like a little boy with problems. Real problems, the kind you don't want any kid to have. I know the look well.

"Fine." I step forward slowly.

"I'm sorry about yesterday." He sprays the antiseptic on my skin. It burns and I grit my teeth. Grover lightly blows on my scrape, his breath making the pain go away. He dabs the Neosporin on my skin. I bite my lower lip, tears welling in my eyes. It's like everything inside of me hurts and feels euphoric at the same time. And I don't know how to control it. I don't know how to feel like this. It was easy with Coop because he made me feel nothing. I'm a rag doll with him. But with Grover, it's as if every one of my senses lights up. Like I'm on fire and covered in water and floating in the air all at the same time.

"Almost done," he says as he unwraps the Band-Aid. "To protect it, so it doesn't break open."

Break open.

That's how this feels.

When I can't take it anymore, I pull back. "Grover, you don't need to save me."

He stands up, putting the first aid stuff back in his pocket. "I want to."

"But you didn't *need* to," I say. I'm my own warrior. I don't need someone else fighting my battles.

"Okay," he says.

"You have . . ." I point at his knees. They're covered in dirt from kneeling on the ground. Without any more words, I bend down in front of Grover, my hand shaking as I reach for him. But I take a deep breath and know what I have to do. I touch him. My skin connects with Grover's skin, and I brush the dirt off of his knee. It's simple and yet not. It's everything.

"Maybe I'm the one who needs saving," he says. When I stand up, he's smiling, the confidence back in his eyes.

"I know you were there last night," I say. "You're there every night, aren't you?"

He nods. "Just in case."

"In case of what?"

"In case she ever decides to jump in," Grover says.

The air in my lungs falls to the ground in a cascade of reality, and I feel like I'm breaking all over again. Grover watches Cassie so he can save *her*.

"Grover, I didn't see you get here." Hayes comes up next to us.

I take a step back, my cheeks on fire, and hand Hayes my granola bar wrapper. "Thanks for the food."

"You're on your way to self-actualization, Durga."

"Something like that," I say.

CHAPTER 14

Cooper,

Molly's birthday is September 16th and I know you saw my mom in the grocery store.

Zander

PS—You're dumped.

"You actually have to step in the water," I say.

"No." Cassie crosses her arms over her chest. "And I'm not wearing that thing."

"You have to," I say.

"I can see the mold growing on it." Cassie points to the orange life vest in my hand.

"You're not allowed in the water without it." I glance at the counselor on duty.

Cassie narrows her eyes. "You look like a lesbian in that swimsuit."

"No, I don't."

"Whatever, Ellen. All I'm saying is that you probably like to eat box. No wonder you're terrible at blow jobs."

"I'm not bad at giving blow jobs!" I yell too loud. Cassie smiles a wicked grin. "And I'm not a lesbian."

"Could have fooled me. I better tell Cleve before he gets too invested."

We stand inches from the waterline of Lake Kimball, Cassie in a hot-pink string bikini and me in my black razorback one-piece. It took forever just to get her off her towel.

"Forget it. You clearly don't want to learn how to swim." I take a step back.

"Fine." Cassie goes back to sit on her towel.

I'm about to walk away and give up when I remember—Cassie makes you hate her so she can be right—that no one cares about her. And I *do* actually care about her or I wouldn't have offered to teach her how to swim. I wouldn't have climbed out the bathroom window and risked getting caught by Madison, or worse, Kerry. I stomp over to her as she sits on her towel.

"Stay here and don't move," I say.

Inside the mess hall, Grover and Bek play an intense game of Speed, their hands slapping cards down on the table with every play. A few other campers are scattered about playing other board games.

"I need your help," I say.

Grover turns to me—I'm clad only in my bathing suit—and says, "This is officially the best day of my life."

I try to cover my body with my arms.

"I need some saltines," I say.

"Why?" Bek asks as he reshuffles his deck.

"Maslow's hierarchy of needs."

"I know Maslow." Bek's eyes stay on the cards. "Great guy."

"Saltines. Can you help me?" I ask Grover.

Grover nods, then disappears behind the kitchen door. I shift back and forth, wishing I'd had the foresight to bring a towel with me.

"Don't worry. You're not my type," Bek says.

"What?"

"The bathing suit. It doesn't do it for me. I've got my eye on someone else." Bek doesn't look up from the cards he's shuffling, but I can tell he's blushing.

"Are we allowed back there?" I ask when Grover returns with an armful of crackers.

"I don't know. I've never asked," Grover says as he hands them to me.

Cassie sits on her beach towel, face up at the sky when I get back. I toss the crackers down on her lap.

"Eat."

"What part of anorexic don't you get, Z?"

"You eat Lemonheads."

"They don't count," she says.

"Why not?"

"Because everyone knows candy isn't *real* food."

"Eat the crackers." I act as resolved as possible considering I'm dealing with a person who might stab me with her stolen fork in my sleep, but she needs to eat. She won't feel safe with me if she doesn't have food.

Cassie picks up a pack. "How many calories are in this thing?"

"Think of it this way—you haven't eaten a proper meal in, like, forever. You're negative thousands of calories. A cracker isn't going to hurt you."

"That's not how calories work, dumb ass."

"Just eat it," I bark.

Cassie sits back on her towel, her lips poised like the next thing that comes out of her mouth is going to be the meanest thing she's ever said. The eating box–blow job comment will be nothing compared to what she has in store for me.

And then she does the unexpected. She unwraps a cracker and eats it.

"What?" she says with a mouthful of food.

"Nothing," I stutter. I guess I shouldn't be surprised at anything when it comes to Cassie.

When she's consumed a few packs of crackers, I ask her again if she wants to learn how to swim.

"Fine." She stands up and dusts off her sandy butt.

"But you have to wear that." I point to the life jacket sitting in the sand.

"Fine, but I call dibs on the first shower when we get back to the cabin."

"Fine," I mock as I clip the life jacket on Cassie. "By the way, I like you on food."

She ignores my comment as we walk down to the shore of Lake Kimball. Cassie stops before stepping in and stares at the water. Lake weed sits in little clumps on the sand. The water is slime green with only a hint of blue, but out in the center of the lake, it's navy.

Minutes go by. And then Cassie says, "I was sent home five times in kindergarten with lice."

"What?"

"Don't make me say it again."

"Five times?" I ask.

"My mom never even gave me a bath. She'd wash me with a washcloth and sprinkle baby powder on my head."

Her big toe hovers over the water.

"Was she afraid of the water or something?"

"I don't know. She didn't talk to me." Cassie looks down at her leg. Her gaze gets strong, like the memories in her head are so present she can't help but acknowledge them.

Her big toe brushes the tip of the water and makes the tiniest ripple.

"Do you want to be like your mom?" I ask.

She shakes her head, so I grab her hand. She doesn't pull away this time.

"Prove it," I say.

We step into the water together.

CHAPTER 15

Dear Mom and Dad,

Will you please send me another bathing suit? I've been spending a lot of time in the water. Don't worry. It's not like it was before. I promise.

And make it a two-piece.

Z

The camp stands divided into two groups on the archery field. The sun hangs low in the sky, which is changing from baby blue to a pink, purple, and orange. At least, the darkness will give my skin a break. Heat radiates off my shoulders from my sunburn. I might have blisters tomorrow. I yawn into my hand, my body sluggish, as Kerry goes over the rules for capture the flag.

"I finally know why you were sent here," Dori whispers to me.

My stomach drops to the ground as I whisper back, "Why?"

She leans toward my ear. "Because clearly you're a masochist."

"I'm not a masochist."

"Then what are you doing with Cassie?" She says it a little too loud and Kerry looks at us.

"Teamwork," Kerry says loudly. "Is essential to success in life. No one can survive on his or her own. *You* are not alone. I want you to remember that when you leave Camp Padua. You are not alone. We need each other. And if you're ever feeling lost, remember it's easier to find yourself if other people help you look." He looks in our direction as he tries to make the game of capture the flag into some team-building activity that's going to help all the lost souls here.

When Kerry looks away, I say to Dori, "It's nothing."

"You stood in the water for three hours and let Cassie make fun of you."

"She wasn't making fun of me." I cross my arms over my chest and fidget uncomfortably in my own skin. I need aloe.

Dori cocks her head to the side. "She wasn't?"

I review some of Cassie's comments from today's swim lesson. Dori is right about the three hours. We stood thigh-deep in the water as Cassie refused to bend down, put her face in the water, and blow bubbles. In the end, Cassie never did it. When the bell rang, she threw her orange life jacket on the beach and left it for me to put away. I tried not to be disappointed, but realized that I wanted to feel disappointed. I got sunburned for nothing.

"It was more like observations," I whisper.

Dori shakes her head at me as Kerry finishes. "One cannot survive on his or her own. Life takes teamwork," he says. He hands out the flags and points out the boundaries for the game. "You can hide your flag anywhere in the woods around the archery field and stables. Please do not leave the area. Any questions?"

A hand in the crowd goes up. I look at the long fingers attached to an even longer arm that's attached to an even longer skinny body. Grover's head sticks up over most of the campers.

"Yes, Grover," Kerry says.

"I have a question."

"Okay."

"I actually have a lot of questions," Grover amends.

"Okay. What about?"

Grover shakes his head. "Girls . . . or should I call them women? That's my first question."

"You should call them women," Kerry says.

"Okay. My first question is about *women*. Why do they smell so good?"

"What does this have to do with the game?" Kerry looks like his patience is waning.

"How am I supposed to play a game when there are women running around smelling so good? I can barely sit next to Zander at dinner without smelling her neck. It's distracting and seems unfair."

Dori looks at me. My sunburned skin gets even hotter.

"I told you," Kerry says. "No boy-girl relationships at camp."

"And I told you, Grover and Zander sounds like a gay couple. No one will know."

"Clearly, Zander is not a boy." Kerry points at me.

"She might be." Cassie pipes up. "Have you seen her bathing suit?"

"Oh, I have." Grover's voice sounds flirty and he wiggles his eyebrows. I cover my face with my hand.

"Back to the questions," Kerry says.

"Technically, Sticks asked a question," Grover says. "So what about the boys who might like boys or the girls who like girls? Are they allowed to have relationships at camp?"

Cassie raises her hand. "What about the girls who think they might be boys having a relationship with boys or girls depending on the day?"

"Yes." Grover points at Cassie. "Which leads me to another question. If a girl thinks she's a boy locked in a girl's body, does she smell like a girl or a boy?"

"You mean *woman*," Cassie says.

"Right. *Woman*," Grover says.

"No relationships whatsoever," Kerry says. "Now, can we please stick to the topic at hand?"

"You asked if I had any questions. I'm just asking them," Grover says innocently.

"About the *game*," Kerry says emphatically.

"The game?" Grover's face looks surprised. "We played it last year. I'm cool. Proceed."

"Thank you." Kerry blows a whistle and campers start to move.

"Grover really likes you," Dori says as our team huddles to make a plan.

"Don't remind me."

"Why do you act like that's a bad thing?" she says.

I don't answer her because I don't know what to say. I get jumbled just thinking about Grover and his colorful feelings mixing with mine. They could potentially make a rainbow or they could make a large mess of brown.

Our team eventually finds a hiding spot high up in a tree, and we stuff our flag there. When the team goes to split into groups, Cassie steps in.

"I'll take it from here." She points around at the group. "You, you, you, not you, you, definitely not you, you, and Zander. You're with me. We'll be in charge of finding the other flag."

Dori pats me on my back as she takes off with the other half of our team and says sarcastically, "Good luck."

I stand, half hunched over as we make a plan to capture the flag.

"Let's split up," Cassie says. She comes up to me and grabs my shoulder. "You're coming with me."

"Ouch." I pull away. "I'm sunburned."

"White-people problems." Cassie shakes her head. "Come on, Z, in the name of teamwork, I need your help."

Cassie proceeds to drag me through the woods, away from the group and the boundaries Kerry set for the game. I try to pull free, but Cassie won't let go of my arm. My ankle still aches a bit and I stumble.

"Where are we going?" I ask, out of breath.

But Cassie doesn't answer; she just pulls on me harder, her nails digging into my skin. When I finally trip on a root sticking out of the ground and fall, she stops.

"What the hell are we doing?" I yell and slam my hand on the ground.

"Aren't you feisty tonight? I told you, I need your help. Consider it a teamwork activity."

"This isn't teamwork," I say. "This is you bossing me around. I tried to help you all day and all you do is make fun of me!"

Cassie stares at me lying on the ground. Her eyes narrow and something different, something I've only seen a few times, flashes in them. Sadness.

"Fine." She starts to walk away.

I groan as I stand up. I don't care if Cassie looks sad that I won't come with her. She can walk away all she wants. I'm done running after her. I'm done standing in the water, waiting for her to make a move. Except . . .

Maybe that's what everyone has done to her. They've left her standing alone in the water because they couldn't take it anymore, and I know what alone feels like.

"Wait," I yell to her. Cassie looks back at me. "I'm coming."

And in that moment, the sadness on her face washes away.

"Just wait out here," she says when we're back at our cabin and she disappears inside. When she comes out, she's wearing the University of Arizona sweatshirt I gave her and carrying her duffel bag.

"Are you running away or something?"

"From what? You can't run away when you're nowhere to start. Come on."

We walk across camp without another word. Cassie seems calm at my side, every once in a while glancing at my burned shoulders. I, on the other hand, look around like a squirrel worried it's going to be hit by a car.

"Would you relax, Z," she says when we get to the Wellness Center. The lights are off inside the wooden building that holds all the medicine needed for kids at camp and who knows what else.

"What are we doing here?" I ask, but Cassie doesn't answer me as she walks up to the locked door and pulls out a key. "Where did you get that?"

"Not telling," she mocks and unlocks the door. "Now stay out here and watch my back."

"Not unless you tell me what you're doing."

"The less you know the better," Cassie says.

"Why?" I bark.

"Innocence, Z. I'm trying to protect you."

I ease back hearing that. "Well, what's so important in the Wellness Center anyway?"

Cassie looks me dead in the eyes. "I'm getting something we need."

She disappears into the building. I pace back and forth looking around for anyone who might come up. What could Cassie need? A million possibilities go through my mind. This is the girl who popped a handful of diet pills the first moment I met her, and I just let her go into a building full of drugs with a duffel bag? I clench my hands at my sides and dig my fingernails into my skin. It hurts. And I don't want to hurt. But I can't stop it like I used to. I can't make it go away.

The second I'm about to go in and get her myself, I hear someone.

I duck behind the side of the building and peek to see who it is. I can feel my heartbeat in my temples as I wait. When a long shadow creeps around the corner followed by a short round one, I ease back.

"What the hell are you guys doing here?" I whisper harshly as I see Grover and Bek.

"Backup." Grover opens his arms like he's inviting me in. When I don't move closer, he leans into me. "Cassie wasn't sure you had the guts." He nudges my side.

"The guts?" I ask.

"Yeah, the guts." Grover says it like he's taunting me. "I told her you did."

I lean back against the building, suddenly exhausted. My legs are tired from standing in the water all day. And Cassie doesn't think I have guts? No one else at this camp would subject themselves to her sarcastic form of torture, except for maybe Grover. I rest my head back against the wall and look up at the darkening sky. Only little patches of color can be seen through the heavy canopy of trees.

"What's the sky like in Arizona?" Grover asks, his soft question surprising me.

"It's big, I guess. Bigger than it is here." I keep my eyes up, trying to find a star through the branches. Our yard doesn't have a single tree in it, just hard grass and dust. Grass is different here. It's smooth, like silk. Like it's not starving for water.

I take a seat on the ground, my body feeling deflated. My voice comes out flat when I say, "Everything's just more exposed in Arizona."

"I think I'd like it." Grover sits next to me.

I shake my head but can't look at him. "You wouldn't."

"Why not?" he asks.

I run my hand over the well-watered, alive grass beside me. "Because everything is one moment away from dying."

I touch the crescent moon indents on my hands that are now fading. The seat of my shorts is starting to feel damp from the rain still soaked in the ground. If I picked up a handful of dirt, it would stick to my palm and fingers. If I did the same in Arizona, it would break into pieces and disappear in the breeze.

As I stare at my hands, I feel something. I glance and catch Grover staring at my neck. A moment later, he catches me catching him. His eyes move down to my sunburn, and Grover touches my shoulder. It stings.

"It hurts," I say.

He nods and rests his hands in his lap.

"I have a question," Bek pipes up. He's pacing in front of us, picking at his nails and looking more nervous than me.

"Just one?" Grover asks.

"What does love feel like?" Bek asks.

"What?" I sit up a bit.

Bek's eyes get wide, the blue center bright. He looks scared. "I think I'm in love."

"Is he lying?" I whisper to Grover.

He shrugs. "It's on my list of questions."

At that moment, Cassie comes flying out of the door. She runs square into Bek, knocking him on his butt. Her duffel bag lands on the ground.

"Sorry, Piglet." She offers him her hand and he takes it. Even in the twilight, I see Bek's cheeks blush.

"Did you get what you need, Sticks?"

Cassie nods at Grover and shakes free from Bek's grip. "Oh my God, your hands are sweaty."

"Je suis désolé," he mumbles. I perk up when I hear the French.

"What?" Cassie asks.

"Nothing." Bek shoves his hands in his pockets and looks at me bug-eyed, like he's begging me not to reveal his secret.

"So what's in the bag?" I reach to grab it off the ground, but Cassie moves in front of me.

"Don't worry about it." She slings it over her shoulder. "Let's get the hell out of here. I need to dump this before anyone sees us."

We half walk, half jog back to our cabin, Bek next to Cassie and Grover next to me. I stare at the duffel bag, wondering what could possibly be in there and at the same time feeling like maybe I don't want to know.

"I almost forgot." Cassie pulls a bottle from her shorts and tosses it at me.

I catch it. "Aloe?" I ask.

"Sorry about your sunburn, Z."

Cassie picks up the pace as she runs ahead with Bek. I stand, holding a full bottle of aloe, shocked.

"Where are you from, Grover?" I finally say.

But he doesn't answer me. When I'm about to ask the question again, Cassie's voice cuts me off.

"Don't waste your time, Z. He'll never tell you."

"Why not?" I ask the question to Grover.

"Did you know that four in ten people never leave the place where they were born?" he says.

I groan at him, too tired and sunburned for his games.

In the cabin, Cassie hides the duffel bag under her bed. Bek takes a long inhale as he stands in the doorway. "It smells like grapes in here."

"See," Grover says. "Girls smell good."

"Is food all you think about, Baby Fat?" Cassie pokes Bek in the stomach.

"And sex." He nods.

"I told you." Grover says to me. "Is this your bed?" He sits down on Molly's quilt.

Why is he allowed to ask so many questions, but when I ask he never answers? He picks up the quilt and inspects the bloodstain from the other night. I run my fingers through my hair and stop myself the second I almost pull a few strands loose. A lump forms in my throat.

"Let's get out of here before we catch one of Mad's STDs." Cassie walks out with Bek behind her.

I wait for Grover to get off my bed, but he doesn't. He runs his hands over my pillow and sits back on my bed, comfortable. I avoid his eyes. He taps on the spot next to him, inviting me to sit down, but I don't move. Instead, I walk into the bathroom and inspect my sunburned shoulders. They're redder than I thought. I rub the cool aloe on them. When Grover comes to stand behind me, I shiver. Maybe from the aloe. Or maybe not.

"It hurts," I say.

He nods. "I know. But it's the only way to heal."

I nod back at him. "That sucks."

"Yes it does," Grover says.

He looks at me in the mirror, his face so calm and even. How does he do that when he's balancing unsteadily on something that might break any second? The thought makes my stomach hurt or maybe my heart break. I can't tell.

"Why won't you tell me where you live?" I ask.

"Because I'm a coward."

"I don't believe that."

"Well, you've got problems," Grover says.

"So do you."

"I acknowledge that," he says.

I do have problems, but I'm working on that. So I tilt my head to the side and hold my hair back, exposing my neck.

"Go ahead," I say.

"Seriously?" Grover asks.

My hands shake. "Yes."

He smiles as he bends down to me. His nose graces my skin, like a feather.

And then Grover smells my neck.

As we walk back to the archery field, he says, "I noticed something."

"What?"

"Cassie has a new sweatshirt."

I shrug. "She does?" I ask.

Grover nods as we crunch over pine needles in the woods.

"How did you and Cassie become friends anyway?" I ask.

"She punched me." A goofy grin sits on Grover's face. "For calling her Sticks."

"But you still call her that."

He takes a step closer to me. "How many nicknames do you think Cassie has?"

"Not many," I say.

"Why do you think that is?" he asks. I look into his wide eyes. There are secrets in him. I can practically see them. "Because no one cares enough to give her one. She needed me to care."

He wipes his fingertips across my aloe-coated shoulder.

"She'll swim," he says. "Don't give up on her."

Don't give up, I repeat in my head.

"Where have you guys been?" Madison comes through the trees, out of breath. "We've been looking for you."

"We've been looking for us, too," Grover says.

"What's that supposed to mean?" Madison asks.

"What *does* that mean, Zander?" Grover looks at me.

Sometimes people are lost because they're too afraid to look at the path. Sometimes people avoid the road for fear of what might be on it. It's easier to stand in the shadows and watch.

"Teamwork." I shrug. "Kerry said if something is lost, it's easier to find it if other people help you look."

And in the dark, I see Grover smile. "Amen."

CHAPTER 16

Aunt Chey,

You're not really my aunt, so let's stop pretending.

Kisses,

Cassie

Cassie puts her head in the water and blows bubbles the next day. She just bends down and does it. I don't have to fight her. She doesn't even snap a sarcastic comment my way. We walk out into Lake Kimball. She looks down at the water and dunks her head.

"There," she says, spitting water out of her mouth and wiping her face.

Shocked, I say, "What the hell did you steal last night?"

"Why?"

"Because this is weird. You're weird. Did you steal drugs from the Wellness Center?"

"Who cares?" Cassie laughs.

"I care," I yell.

A half smile creeps up on Cassie's face. "Why do you care?"

I look down at the T-shirt covering my bathing suit. I need it to protect my shoulders today. They can't get any more sun or blisters will form. The aloe helped but it didn't fully heal them overnight. It will take a few days.

"I realized something last night." I play with the bottom of my shirt.

"What?"

"I haven't conjugated a French verb in three days."

"What does that have to do with me?" Cassie asks.

I gnaw on my bottom lip. I can't remember a time in the past year when I haven't had a constant stream of foreign words running through my head, like a sea of letters I could dive into and disappear. But Cassie makes everything hard. She breaks the words to pieces until they're too broken to read. Or maybe I'm broken. But now I don't feel like putting the words back together.

"I don't want you to get kicked out of camp, okay?" I say.

"Why? Because you'd feel bad for me?"

"No," I snap. "Because I'd feel bad for *me*." Cassie narrows her eyes, like she's trying to see past my lie, but it's not a lie. It's the truth. "And I'd feel bad for Grover, too," I say.

When I say his name, Cassie's face gets serious. "You don't have to worry. I didn't steal drugs."

"Good."

"But what if I did." Cassie invades my space. She leans in close, examining my eyes. "What would you do?"

This is a test. I can feel it.

"Nothing," I say.

Cassie gives me a smart-ass look and eases back.

"I put my head in the water. What comes next?" she asks.

"Floating," I say, taking a breath. "You need to be able to float to swim."

Cassie yanks on the orange life jacket around her neck. "This makes me float, dumb ass."

An angry comment. Confirmation she really isn't on drugs. I drag Cassie by the life jacket back to shore and grab the packet of crackers from my pocket that Grover handed me under the table at breakfast.

"Eat." I hand them to her.

"Only with a side of diet pills." She scans my body. "You need them, too."

"No diet pills."

"Yes diet pills," Cassie says.

"No diet pills," I say. Cassie's rigid stance doesn't change. "I promise I won't conjugate any French verbs as long as you don't take any pills."

"How do I know if you're really doing it?"

"You won't. You have to believe that I'll tell you the truth."

"The truth," Cassie repeats. And then she says, "Fine. I won't take any diet pills if you tell me why you were sent here."

Cassie's words surprise me. For the whisper of a moment, I see one sentence of the French imperfect in my head. My French teacher made us all go around the classroom and talk about something we repeatedly did when we were younger, using the tense.

Quand j'étais petite, nous allions à la plage chaque semaine.

When I was young, we used to go to the beach every week.

She clicked her tongue on the roof of her mouth and told me that was impossible. There's no beach nearby. She was right. I made it up, but I didn't want to talk about the habitual stuff we did. She knew what my family did anyway. Everyone knew.

"I'll tell you." I can't look at Cassie. "But not yet."

"You promise?"

I force my eyes up. "Do you promise not to take any more diet pills?"

Cassie's head moves up and down hesitantly. "I promise," she says.

We shake on it. I look at the hideous life jacket around her neck. "Now what do we do about that?"

A wicked grin grows across Cassie's face. "I'll take care of it."

Cassie puts her head under the water many more times before the bell rings to end our activities. I teach her how to kick. She holds on to the side of the H dock in the red zone making waves with her legs, her head in the water, and blowing bubbles. Every time younger kids swim past, she splashes them and smiles. By the end of the day, she's lying on her back, face toward the sun, and floating in her life jacket.

I sit on my butt in Lake Kimball, feeling the sand and water between my fingers, and watch her. My shirt billows out in front of me like a heavy water balloon. It weighs me down.

Cassie watches me as I walk to the end of the dock. With the sun on the water, I can see the drop-off that marks the yellow zone from green. The sandy bottom disappears and all that's left is navy blue.

When I dive in, my shirt drags as I push my way through the water. I touch the bottom with my hand just to know it's there. There is a bottom. Looking up through the blue, I push my feet off the ground and start fighting my way back to the top. My shirt clings to the water, like a million tiny hands pulling on me, trying to make me go back down, but I don't want to be on the bottom anymore. It's dark down there. And I don't want to fight so hard to breathe. Breathing should be easy.

When my head comes above the surface moments later, Cassie yells from the shallow end, "Show-off!"

We gather our things and head up the stairs toward the mess hall. Water drips off Cassie's hair and down her back. The ridges of her shoulders and spine stick out; she's so skinny. I don't know how her parents look at her every day and don't help. My mom would be all over me.

A sinking feeling overtakes my stomach. I swallow hard and ask her, "Do you still live with your mom?"

I see Cassie's bones pull in tight. "Why?"

I try to act casual and even. "Just wondering."

"No." Cassie picks up the pace, but I follow closely.

"Who do you live with now?"

She whips around. "I did what you asked. I blew bubbles. Don't burst mine with your questions."

She stomps her way to the top of the stairs, but I stay put. My stomach is sour with sadness. I hate sadness. Anything is better than sadness. Even feeling nothing.

I look down and count the steps as I make my way up the stairs. At the top, a pair of large feet stops my movement.

"I have a package," Grover says.

"What?"

"Do you want my package?"

I look down at the zipper on his shorts. I can't help it. For a breath, I imagine what's underneath. Grover is just so long.

He pulls a brown box from behind his back. "My package for you." He smiles. "It's not actually from me. I'm just the delivery boy."

I take it from him.

"Delivery *man*, I should say." Grover puffs out his thin chest, and the image that was in my head moments ago is back. My cheeks heat instantly.

"Thanks." I start to walk away.

"She did it," Grover says. "I told you she would."

And he did. But that's not what I want Grover to tell me.

"By the way." I glance at the return address on the package. My address.

"Yes?" he asks.

"I don't have a boyfriend anymore."

"My heightened mental and emotional state just elevated." Grover looks down at his package. "Along with other things."

"Gross." I shake my head as I walk away. Because it is gross. Kind of. Maybe. I take one more look over my shoulder at Grover. Okay. Maybe not.

CHAPTER 17

Dear Mom,

It's humid in Michigan. Humidity is weird. The air holds on to all that water and doesn't let it come pouring out. I think I'm humid and you want me to be dry like Arizona. But Arizona air doesn't have anything in it. It actually sucks the life out of your skin until you're chapped and cracking. Maybe we could meet in the middle? Iowa, maybe. Or Nebraska.

I don't think my friend Cassie has an address.

I'm sad about that.

I'm sad.

I'm sad.

I'm sad.

I know you wanted a longer letter. I hope this helps.

Thanks for the two-piece.

Z

I wake up to tapping on my forehead, like water dripping down from the ceiling. I know this feeling. When I open my eyes, Cassie is inches above my face.

"I'm ready to float," she whispers.

"It's the middle of the night."

"No shit, Z. Get up." Cassie's wearing my sweatshirt and shorts, but tied around her neck I can see her hot-pink bathing suit. She holds up my new two-piece. "Finally."

I snatch it from her as I get out of bed.

Cassie works open the window in the bathroom as I quietly slide into my bathing suit. Madison sleeps curled up in the fetal position. The silver key dangles from her neck.

"Do you think you'd sneak out if we weren't locked in?" I ask Cassie in a whisper.

"What?"

"It's like in France—they let their kids drink from an early age, and it's not a big deal. But we don't do that here. We don't let kids drink, so they want it more."

Cassie rolls her eyes. "I thought you were over the whole French thing."

"It's just an analogy." I glance back at the locked door. "But I don't think I would."

"Would what? I got bored the second you said France."

"If the door wasn't locked, I don't think I'd care about sneaking out. Would you?"

Cassie must get what I'm trying to say because her face becomes sullen and serious.

"Everyone wants to find a way out when they're locked in. What most people don't realize is that there's always another locked door." Cassie stares forward like she's trying to burn a hole through the wall with her eyes and then snaps out of it. "Let's get the hell out of here."

She escapes first. As I'm wiggling my way through the window, I glance back at the girls sleeping in the cabin. I freeze when Hannah moves in her bed, shifting from one side of her body to the other so she's facing the bathroom. She smacks her lips a few times and nuzzles down into the sheets, but her eyes never open.

At the lake, Cassie strips down to her bikini. I hesitate for a second. It's been a while since my stomach has been exposed. Maybe it's been forever—I can't remember.

"What are you waiting for, Z?" Cassie barks in a whisper. "No one's gonna see you."

But Cassie doesn't know who might be watching. I scan the trees for Grover and strip down to my suit.

We wade out into the lake. I scoop a handful of cold water and drip it on my shoulders. It feels like an ice pack.

"Ok, I got us here. Now, teach me."

"Have you had any diet pills?"

Cassie grinds her teeth. "No." She grabs her sides. "I can feel the fat clinging to my skin already. It's gonna make me sink."

"Heavy people float just fine."

"Are you saying I'm heavy?"

I ignore the door Cassie just opened for a rigged fight. I'd lose. "I'm going to teach you two different ways to float—one on your back and one on your stomach."

Cassie jumps up and down in the water. "Let's just get to it. I'm freezing my fat ass off."

I watch how comfortable she is in the water now. She wouldn't put her toe in last week. Seeing water all around her, that doesn't seem possible.

"What happened with your mom?" I ask.

Cassie stops jumping.

"Administrators tend to check the situation at home when you come to school with a gash on your leg and a bad case of lice for the fifth time. It was over after that."

"So your mom lost custody of you?"

"She didn't lose anything." Cassie squeezes her hands into fists at her side and her knuckles crack. "You can't lose something you don't want to begin with. She just gave up."

"My parents are the opposite. They hold on too tight." I brush my fingers over the top of the water.

"Boohoo for you. Your parents care about you," Cassie mocks.

I swallow hard. "I didn't say I was the one my parents held on to."

"Your dead sister?" Cassie asks.

The breeze blows, shaking the leaves on the trees. They sound like whispers in the night. I look at the shoreline and up at the mess hall. A dim light is on in the building. It catches the shadow of someone sitting on the top of the stairs.

"Grover says I'm the same way. That I hold on to things."

Cassie looks at me, her eyes practically burning in the moonlight. "Teach me how to float."

We walk deeper into the lake, and I tell Cassie to lie on her back. She tells me I'm fucking crazy. I tell her that's no secret; we're at a camp for crazy kids. She corrects me and says it's a camp for kids with heightened mental and emotional states. Then I tell her that I'll hold her up. That I won't let her sink.

"Promise?" she asks.

"Promise."

She lies flat on the water.

I keep her steady with my arms under her back. After a few minutes, I say, "I'm going to take one arm away."

In the dark, her hair and skin blend in with the black water. They look like one body. Cassie is of the water and the water is of Cassie. When she nods, I take my one arm away.

She stays still on top of the water. I smile down at her.

"You'll never have lice again," I say.

She looks at me with hard eyes. "Stop holding on so damn tightly."

I take my other arm away, and Cassie floats by herself. She didn't give up.

And I let go.

As we walk quietly back to the cabin, Cassie pulls a box of Lemonheads out of her sweatshirt and offers me some. It's her sweatshirt now, a fact that makes me happy, truly happy.

I swirl the sugarcoated candies around in my mouth, careful not to bite into them. I don't want to eat too fast. It's better when they dissolve on their own. Longer and better.

"My mom is afraid I'm going to die," I finally say when we get back to the girls' side of camp.

Cassie looks at me. Her face doesn't hold a judgment, at least not on the surface.

"I'd say *every* mom is afraid of her kid dying, but my mom wouldn't give a shit if I died."

"That makes me sad," I say.

"It makes me angry."

I look down at the ground. "It made *me* angry that my mom is so afraid of me dying."

Cassie shoves my shoulder. "Now, *that* makes me sad," she says, and then she's silent for a while.

"Tell me something about your sister," she eventually says.

I take a shaky breath. The request is unexpected. "I could hear her in her room down the hall from me, just breathing. It put me to sleep every night. Like a really fucked-up lullaby," I say. "And I miss it. I miss it a lot."

"But you're not mad anymore."

I shake my head. "And you swam tonight."

She smiles. "Say it again."

"You swam tonight." Now it's my turn to be silent. Cassie pats my burned shoulders. I've never been happier to *feel* my sunburn. "What do we have if we don't have hope?" I ask.

Cassie laughs. "Reality."

"But maybe sometimes what we hope for becomes a reality."

"Maybe," she says.

The reality is that Molly is dead.

And it hurts.

I will die.

And it hurts.

Breathing is life.

And it hurts.

All life ends.

And it hurts.

I need to live.

Even if it hurts.

"Shit." Cassie's voice surprises me.

"What?"

"The window." Her voice shakes. "The window is closed." Cassie points to our cabin.

"Shit," I say and run my hands through my hair. The moment before I pull a few strands loose, Cassie stops me.

"When the door opens, sneak into the crowd," she says.

"What?"

"Act like you were asleep the whole time." Cassie takes off her Arizona sweatshirt and hands it to me. Her hot-pink bathing suit lights up in the dark.

"What are you going to do?"

"Put it on. Act sleepy."

“What are you going to do?” I say louder.

Cassie smiles. “You taught me how to swim, right?” She pushes me toward the shadows of the cabin. “It’s called teamwork, Z.”

She starts singing then. “She’ll Be Comin’ Round the Mountain” echoes between the cabins as she runs, knocking on doors, and waking everyone up.

TRUST

CHAPTER 18

Dear Mom and President Cleveland,

It is a fact that we will all be a statistic some day. Did you know that the odds of drowning are one in 1,073? I now know a girl who will not be that statistic.

Your son,

Grover Cleveland

Cassie is placed in solitary for a week. She has to sit with Kerry and the counselors at all meals, where she is still only eating with a spoon and knife, and sleep in Kerry's personal cabin with Madison, while he sleeps in one of the boys' cabins. A "counselor in training" named Anne, who's a sophomore premed major and who most days assists the nurse doling out medicine, sleeps in our cabin.

The first day Cassie isn't with me, I swim down at the lake in the afternoon, until it starts to rain. When Kerry hears a crack of thunder, he makes us all get out and tells us to find another activity, preferably one inside, but I sneak back to the cabin.

It's extra musty as I listen to the plunk of rain on the roof and stare at Cassie's empty bed. I put her sweatshirt on it. She'll need it when she gets back. I flip through the *Seventeen* magazine I brought to camp. The cover is gone and the humidity has made the pages wavy and crinkle when I open it. I turn to the article on how to flirt without being obvious and read the list of rules.

Keep eye contact.

Don't play with your hair.

Act confident.

Smile.

Show off your neck.

This is ridiculous. I close the magazine. I don't like that Cassie isn't here. I feel alone, a feeling I used to like, but not really anymore.

I walk over to her bed and touch the bare mattress.

Inside the mess hall, campers gather around an old television, watching a movie. I find Grover sitting at the back of the group. Cassie is tucked in the corner, her arms crossed, as she sits between Kerry and Hayes. She looks tortured.

I sneak up and sit behind Grover. His tall torso blocks my view of the screen, and he's wearing a bright blue tank top. I can see all the bones that run along his shoulders and collarbone. His skin is golden from being out in the sun.

I lean in a bit and smell the coconut sunscreen on his skin.

Grover turns around with a wicked grin on his face. He knew I was behind him.

I motion toward the door, and, quietly, we sneak out of the mess hall, but I steal a look at Cassie before the door closes. She gives me the middle finger. I do the same back. We both smile and I feel better already.

Grover and I stand in the rain for a moment as I play with my hair, unable to look at him. I try to remember the rules to flirting. I'm pretty sure I just broke them all. I finally blurt out, "What movie is playing?"

"*The Breakfast Club*."

"I've never seen it. Is it good?" I ask.

Grover shrugs. "It just started."

A raindrop hangs seconds from dripping off of Grover's chin. I watch it as it collects more water and gets heavy. The moment when I think I'll reach up and wipe it away, it falls to the ground. I stand in the rain, disappointed yet again.

"Do you want to go back inside?" I ask.

He shakes his head.

"It's wet out here," I say.

"I don't care," he says. "Do you care?"

I do care, about so many things I didn't before, but not about the rain. "I'm starting to," I say.

"Follow me then." Grover smiles.

We walk down to the beach. I slip off my flip-flops and feel the wet sand between my toes. I even wiggle them around so I can feel every grain stuck on my skin. But when Grover moves to step onto the dock, I grab his arm.

"Probably not the best place to be during a thunderstorm."

"You're right. The experience could be shocking. Did you know the odds of us getting hit by lightning are one in seven hundred thousand?" He steps onto the dock.

"Did Bek tell you that?" I ask.

Grover looks at me over his shoulder. "The odds are in our favor. Not to be struck by lightning, that is. Other odds, not so much."

"I'm pretty sure the odds increase when you're on a metal dock."

"This is probably true." Grover motions for me to join him on the death trap. But I guess all of life is a death trap, so I follow him. We sit down on the end and he puts his feet in the water.

"So what odds aren't in your favor?" I ask.

Grover's wet hair sticks to his forehead and he wipes it back as he gets out his notebook. He flips to a page and holds his hand over it to protect the paper from the rain. "The odds of dating a millionaire: one in 215. Not bad. The odds of winning an Academy Award: one in 11,500. Still more probable than lightning."

"Wow." I put my feet in the water next to him. Raindrops splash around us and on the surface of Lake Kimball, making it murky.

"The odds of writing a *New York Times* bestseller: one in 220. The odds of being in a car accident: one in 18,585." I watch Grover read from his notebook. He doesn't look at me. "The odds of getting arthritis: one in seven. The odds of dying from heart disease: one in three."

"These are all general statistics. I asked what odds aren't in *your* favor?" I say.

"The odds of getting cancer: one in two," he says. "That's not good for anyone."

"Grover, tell me something about you."

He looks out across the lake. Houses and cabins line the shore across from us—it all looks so normal, but Grover doesn't. For a moment, he seems like a lost kid longing for one of those houses to be his reality.

Then he seems to snap back together. He looks down at his notebook.

"The odds of becoming president: one in ten million. Did you know Grover Cleveland was one of the fattest presidents?"

"I don't want to know about *that* Grover Cleveland. I want to know about you," I say.

"But the president was *way* more interesting. For starters, his real name wasn't even Grover, it was Stephen."

"I don't want to know about the president!" I yell.

"You're mad. I can tell. That's good. Mad is good. You're finally acknowledging how you feel."

I grab Grover's hand. "I want to know how *you* feel."

"You're touching me right now, so I'm feeling warm in inappropriate places."

I drop his hand, like it's something gross. It's not. But I feel his pain and I know he feels it, too.

When I stand up on the dock, he looks at me.

"Tell me why you won't eat apples," he says.

"We're not talking about me."

"You are so much more interesting. And Molly, tell me something about her," Grover says. A crack of thunder rolls overhead.

"What are you afraid of?" I say slowly.

"Well, that sounded close, so right now, I'm kind of afraid the odds of getting struck by lightning just went up."

"Fuck the odds," I say.

"I love it when you talk dirty." Grover smiles, but it doesn't reach his eyes. I stay silent as thunder rumbles through the sky and the upturned corners of his mouth fade into a straight line. His lip quivers in the rain. "The odds of being schizophrenic when you have a schizophrenic parent: one in ten," he says. He doesn't read that one out of his notebook. It's memorized.

The air is pushed out of my lungs like someone just punched me.

"Fuck the odds," I say again. I hold out my hand for him to take as thunder rolls above us.

He looks at my palm.

Rain falls between us.

"I can't," Grover says. "I can't." He leaves me on the end of the dock to fight the odds alone.

I look out at the gray water. It doesn't look dangerous.

"Durga, Durga, Durga," I say.

I strip off my clothes and dive in.

CHAPTER 19

Dear Mom and Dad,

Odds are I will probably die of cancer or heart disease even if I eat spinach. Because everyone dies. And spinach leaves a film on my teeth. I hate the film.

I've stopped eating spinach.

Z

Kerry runs down to the beach and yells for me to "get out of the water this instant." A group of campers stands on the deck of the mess hall watching.

"Are you trying to get killed?" he screams.

"No. But the odds of dying are one in one."

"Have you lost your mind?" Kerry's anger seethes through his clenched teeth.

"That's why I'm here, right?"

Kerry glares at me. "Get your things and head back to your cabin to change for dinner."

I collect my clothes from the end of the dock and notice something next to my shirt. Grover's notebook and pen. I flip to the back page and start scribbling.

When I see him at dinner, I set the notebook down on the table. "You left this on the dock."

"Finding my lost items. Thank you." But Grover doesn't look at me. Those are the only words he says all night.

The rain lasts into the evening, forcing us to stay in our cabins after dinner. Dori asks if she can paint my toenails. Hannah and Katie listen to music and write letters home. Counselor in training Anne reads a book with a half-naked guy on the cover, and I can't stop staring at Cassie's empty bed as Dori puts cotton between my toes.

"What color?" Dori asks.

"Huh?" Cassie's pillowcase has a hole in it, so do her sheets around the edges. She's been sleeping in rags.

"What color?" Dori holds up her bag full of different-colored nail polish.

"You pick."

Dori paints them red. I barely notice. When she's done, I waddle—my toes separated and pointing toward the ceiling so they don't smudge—with Molly's quilt in my arms over to Cassie's bed. I don't know what the odds are for having a sister die, but it doesn't matter anymore. I lay the quilt down, so Cassie can use it when she gets back. Then I look at each girl in the cabin. Someone did this. Someone closed the window.

The next day, breakfast with Grover is as awkward as dinner was. Bek tells us that he's the reincarnation of Paul McCartney.

"Paul isn't dead," Grover says.

"That's what you think." Bek speaks with a mouthful of food. "He was shot by that guy in Central Park."

"That was John Lennon."

"That's what you think," Bek says again.

"No." Grover says. "That's what *you* think."

"That *is* what I think," Bek counters.

"Correct."

"Correct." Bek nods. "I think I'm choking. Can someone give me a Heimlich?"

"Who cares? You'll just get reincarnated again," Grover says.

"Good point." Bek pretends to die and come back as Justin Timberlake.

In group share-apy, Cassie looks tired, or maybe she's well rested because she can't sneak out in the middle of the night like she's been doing. But the scowl on her face would say otherwise.

"Why is trust so important?" Madison says, as she walks around the circle. No one says anything, just like always. "Come on, ladies," she groans.

Hannah sits pigeon-toed staring at her feet and rubbing her covered arms, like she wants to curl up in a ball and disappear. Katie leans her face up toward the sun, closing her eyes. Cassie has one leg up on the bench and is picking dirt out from under her toenails and wiping it on her shorts.

Dori finally raises her hand and takes St. Anthony from Madison. "Trust makes you feel secure."

"Exactly."

"That's total bullshit," Cassie pipes up.

"Why do you think that?" Madison asks, handing the St. Anthony statue to Cassie.

"Trust only gives you the illusion of security," Cassie says.

"So you can never fully trust anyone?" Dori asks.

"You trusted your mom and she still married an asshole," Cassie offers.

Dori sits back in her seat. "That's true."

"See. Trust is a scam created by authority." Cassie points at Madison. "Mads would like us to think she wants what's best for us, but what she really wants is to get experience for grad school and do it with an older man this summer."

"That's not true, Cassie. I do care."

"Please, I see how you look at Kerry." Cassie rolls her eyes.

"Please do not start down this path, Cassie," Madison says.

"Start down this path? I was born on this path. Nobody gave me a choice where to start."

"That may be true, but you have a choice where you go."

"I do?" Cassie says sarcastically. "The problem with trust is that it's a scam. If you don't trust anyone, you won't get hurt."

"People are human, Cassie. They make mistakes," Madison says.

"And you want me to trust people who make mistakes?"

"No one is perfect."

"What mistakes have you made, Mads?" Cassie glares at her, intrigued. "Huh? Why are we the ones always sharing? Why don't you share your dirty little secrets with the group?"

Madison looks around startled and unable to speak, her face turning pale. Cassie sits back savoring the moment, but I can't join her. For a moment, Madison actually looks broken—broken like we're all broken. When she regains her composure, Madison puts her counselor persona back on and says, "This isn't about me. Without trust, we lose faith. If we lose faith, we lose hope, and without hope, what do we have?"

"Reality," Cassie bites.

"You're just afraid," Hannah says. She doesn't look at Cassie when she says it. Her eyes focus on the hole she's digging in the ground with her shoe. Hannah doesn't see Cassie's eyes get big. I can practically witness the fire ignite in her brain. She walks over to Hannah and puts her leg up on the bench so her scar is close to Hannah's face.

"You're damn right I'm afraid, Razor Blades. And you're a pussy." Cassie touches Hannah's long-sleeved shirt. "You probably use your shaving razor to slice up these arms. Would you like me to introduce you to someone who can do that for you?"

Hannah shakes her head.

"You should be afraid, too." Cassie turns back to the group, her eyes wilder than usual. As I watch her, I know something is off. "Trust? Faith? Hope? Those are pretty words to make us feel better about reality. But the world is not pretty. Hannah is not pretty with her cut-up arms. Katie is not pretty with her burned-out puke fingers. Dori is not pretty in general. And we still don't know why Zander isn't pretty other than her odd obsession with French people."

"And what about you?" Dori asks.

Cassie's shoulders fall. "I'm the ugliest of them all because I can't pretend. I can't wear a shirt to cover my scars or duck into the bathroom every time I want to puke the ugly out of me. I don't have a choice. It's all over me. That might be the only thing you *can* trust."

"Please sit down now, Cassie," Madison says.

"Gladly." She fakes a smile and curtsies. Cassie drops the St. Anthony figurine in the dirt and presses her heel into it before taking her seat.

Madison decides to change directions with the session and lines us up to do an activity. She hands everyone a blindfold.

"We're going to do a 'trust walk' through the woods with a partner."

Dori rolls her eyes. "This should be great."

Madison explains that one person will be blindfolded and lead the other through the woods with only verbal cues from their partner as to where to go. The second she gives that direction, every girl takes a giant step away from Cassie. I'm sure none of them have taken the time to look at Cassie's bed. And I may not know what's going on with her today, but I know enough, so I take a step closer to her. Cassie makes a face like she's annoyed—like she wants to be alone.

But I stay put.

"What's going on? Did you eat today?" I ask.

"Like you care," Cassie snaps.

"I do care."

"Just put your blindfold on, Z. Or don't you trust me?" Cassie says it like she's challenging me. I groan, not because I'm nervous, but because I'm annoyed.

With the blindfold on, my other senses light up. I can hear laughter echoing up from campers swimming in the lake and the wind ruffle the leaves on the trees. I put my arms out in front of me and run my hands through the empty air. I even open my mouth to taste it. Everything is humid and smells like pine.

"You look like Helen Keller." Cassie's voice comes through the dark.

I drop my arms. "Shut up."

"Trust is essential to success in life," Madison says. "You have to *trust* others. But most importantly, you have to trust yourself."

"Bullshit," I hear Cassie say under her breath.

Cassie's first instruction is for me to take five steps forward. When I do it, I run into a tree. My foot hits first and then my head.

"I said four steps, not five," Cassie says.

She tells me to turn to the right and follow her voice.

"Keep coming. Keep coming," she says over and over. I hold out my arms and walk in the direction that I think is toward her.

I trip on a log and fall on my face.

"Cassie!" I yell, still blindfolded but lying on the ground. "You're supposed to tell me if something is in the way."

"I didn't see that," she says.

I touch the thing I fell over. "You didn't see a gigantic tree trunk?"

"Sorry, Z. Geez, don't you trust me?"

I stand up and dust dirt off of my knees, but I don't desert her. I won't. Not now. Not after what she did. She sacrificed herself for me. I don't have a single friend who's ever done that.

"Next direction, please," I say.

Cassie tells me to walk straight. When I don't run into anything or trip, my shoulders relax.

"Turn to your left."

I do it and walk forward.

"Now, make a slight right."

I'm still clear. Not even a stick cracks under my feet.

"Take seven steps forward."

I start counting in my head. One. Step. Two. Step. Three. A branch catches on the sleeve of my shirt. I unhook myself. I step forward. Four. Step. Five. Step. A branch or stick scratches my leg.

"Shit," I whisper to myself and feel my leg. A swollen scrape has already bubbled on my skin.

"You okay, Z?"

That actually hurt a little, but I stand up straight.

"Peachy," I say.

"Two more steps."

Six. Step. Seven . . .

The second my foot hits the ground I hear it—buzzing. A lot of buzzing. I feel something close to me and then something else. I rip off my blindfold and look up. A hornets' nest dangles above me, and Cassie stands yards away with a wicked smile on her face.

"Fuck!" I scream and flail my arms to prevent getting stung.

"I think you're supposed to stand still," Cassie hollers.

I bolt away from the nest and over to Cassie, jumping and checking my clothes for any hornets that may be hiding in my T-shirt, ready to sting me.

"What is wrong with you?" I say through heavy breaths. I can feel my heartbeat in my toes.

"I thought we covered this. What *isn't* wrong with me?"

"What if I was allergic to hornets or something? You could have killed me!" I swat at my clothes one more time.

"If it isn't me, it will be something else. We all die, Z."

"Real nice, Cassie. God, I thought we were friends. But you know what, fuck you." I drop the blindfold on the ground.

"No. Fuck you," Cassie says, her face changing from amused to stone. The moment I'm ready to storm away, she surprises me and asks, "Why are your toes painted?"

I look down at my flip-flops. "Dori did it last night."

Her face gets tight. "You know what? Fuck you."

"What?" I ask totally confused.

"Are you having sex with Cleve? No, don't answer that. Fuck you." Cassie starts to walk away quickly.

I run after her, trying to understand the meaning behind all the *fuck yous*. "I'm not having sex with Grover."

She stops still and I almost run into her boney chest. "His name is Cleve. *Cleve.* I see how you two look at each other," Cassie says. "But he was my friend first."

"He still is," I say.

She shakes her head. "And now Dori? *Dori?* The Beano fart girl? You know what? Just . . . whatever, Dutch Oven." Cassie stomps off.

I stand, shocked, watching Cassie slam her feet into the ground, and then I get it. I run up and grab her arm. "Just because I let Dori paint my nails doesn't mean I care about you any less. That's not how friendship works."

Cassie squints at me, seemingly contemplating what I've said, and my heart breaks again for her as I wonder if Cassie has ever had a meaningful relationship in her life. She looks at my feet. "You should have picked orange anyway. It's more you."

"You're probably right."

"You're damn right, I'm right."

We still don't move. Cassie looks around like she's annoyed she's standing here with me, but at this point I know her well enough to know that if she wanted to leave, she'd do it.

"I never thanked you for what you did," I say.

"What are you talking about?" Cassie exaggerates the words as she says them. I cock my head at her. She knows damn well what I'm talking about.

I walk back and pick up the blindfold, swinging it around on my finger. "It's your turn now." Cassie hesitates for a moment and snatches it from me, like she's not afraid of what I might do. "Maybe we can paint each other's toes later. Clearly, I need a new color," I say.

I lead Cassie into three trees and one gigantic mud puddle, but she doesn't take the blindfold off. Not when she bonks her head. Not when she stubs her toe. Not when she's covered in mud. Not once.

"What the hell happened to you?" Madison asks when we return to the Circle of Hope.

"I told you, Mads," Cassie says. "Trust will beat the shit out of you." But the smile is back on Cassie's face. We walk away together in search of the perfect toenail color.

CHAPTER 20

Aunt Chey,

Please don't pass on my letters to the school like you did last year.

I said please.

Kisses,

Cassie

Cassie plops her tray down and takes a seat at our table for breakfast a few days later. Grover and I are continuing our awkward silence, but Cassie manages to break it. She picks up her glass of water and takes a sip. Grover, Bek, and I stare at her. It's a relief to have her back.

On her tray is a pile of scrambled eggs and a piece of toast.

"Sticks," Grover says in a serious tone.

"What?"

"Don't freak out, but a carbohydrate is sitting on your plate. Do you need me to kill it for you?"

She rolls her eyes. "Zander's eating a pig."

"I'm sick of oatmeal." I steal a quick glance at Grover. He hasn't taken his notebook out since I gave it back to him.

"I'm sick." We all look at Bek as he shovels a bagel in his mouth.

"Duh, Baby Fat. You're sick in the head." Cassie rolls her eyes. "We've got more important things to discuss than food."

"Nothing is more important than food." Grover gestures to his tray. "This is the doorway to everything."

"Sex is important." Bek takes another bite.

"I wonder what Maslow says about sex?" Grover says to Bek.

"Who the fuck is Maslow and why does everyone keep talking about him?" Cassie pokes at her eggs.

"He's my dead uncle," Bek says. "He kind of invented gravity."

Cassie fills her spoon and drops a small amount of eggs into her mouth. I don't think she chews. "Back to the important things," she says.

Grover wags his finger at her. "Nothing is more important than food and sex."

"Is that all you think about?" I ask.

"Yes," both the boys say at the same time. It's the only word Grover has spoken in my direction in days.

Cassie leans in toward the center of the table and motions for us to huddle together. Grover's leg brushes up against mine and our knees touch. I wonder what he's thinking about at this exact moment. The odds would point to sex or food or both, but then he pulls away. And I'm disappointed again.

"It's Black Out Night," Cassie says.

"What does that mean?" I whisper.

"It means it's time," she says.

"Time for what?" I ask.

"The duffel bag."

Grover smiles and Bek looks totally calm when Cassie says the words, but everything inside of me gets tight.

"I'll bring it down to the lake this afternoon and stash it in the back of the equipment shed behind the life jackets," Cassie says.

"Why?" I ask.

"God, you ask a lot of questions, Z."

"Just tell me."

"Just trust me," Cassie barks.

"Fine." I cross my arms and sit back in my seat.

"Cassie," a voice rings across the mess hall. We all look up at the same time to find Kerry pointing at an empty chair next to him at the counselors' table. "You have to sit with us."

Cassie doesn't move. She doesn't even look at Kerry. Slowly every eye in the room lands on her, but she just sits back in her seat, grabs a chunk of her hair, and starts braiding it so that it's sticking straight up in the air.

"So your uncle invented gravity?" she asks Bek. He nods.

"Cassie," Kerry says again.

She grabs another section and braids. "I thought God invented gravity."

"My uncle is God," Bek says. "I just don't like to tell people because then they treat me differently."

"Why did your uncle God make you so fat?"

"He died before he could tell me." Bek pats his stomach.

"Cassie," Kerry yells one last time.

She finally looks at him. The two braids resemble antennae. "What?"

"Your seat." Kerry points aggressively at the chair.

"I'm busy talking to Bek about his uncle God. But thank you for the offer."

"I'm not offering. I'm telling you," Kerry says.

"And I'm telling you that I already have a seat."

"Cassie, please take *this* seat."

"God, Kerry, you sound kind of desperate for me to sit with you."

"Please don't take the Lord's name in vain," he says.

"I think you mean Bek's uncle's name in vain. And I'm pretty sure he doesn't give a shit about me because he already knows I'm going to hell. What do you think, Bek?"

"You're probably going to hell," Bek says.

"See."

"Cassie. Sit down," Kerry says through tight teeth.

"Jesus Christ, Kerry, you're pushy. I bet Uncle God doesn't approve of that."

"Cassie!" He pulls out the chair. "Sit here."

Cassie rolls her eyes and gets up. She stretches her arms over her head and yawns. Her tank top rises so high the whole room can see her stomach and ribs. I can't tell if she's gained any weight, though it doesn't look that way. But there are bite marks on her toast, and only half of the eggs are left on her tray.

"Cassie!"

"Okay. Okay. Jesus Christ."

"Cassie!"

"Goddamn it, Kerry. Give me a second."

Cassie shoots the table a grin, and I push her tray toward her. She needs to finish her toast.

"Don't forget about tonight. You have to come," she says. "Please." Cassie makes her way over to the counselors' table, her braids bobbing as she walks.

When the bell rings for our first activity, Cassie's tray still sits on our table, so I clean it up. A pit forms in my stomach when the toast goes into the garbage can. But there's always tomorrow.

"Are you staying for arts and crafts, Durga?" a voice says behind me.

I turn to find Hayes with an armful of newspapers. He sets them down on a table.

"I don't know," I say.

"It's okay not to know." He goes to one of the cabinets along the wall and pulls out a bucket. "It's hard for people to admit that they don't know something. But the truth is that life isn't about getting the right answers. It's about asking the right questions." He fills the bucket with water from the faucet.

"I guess I'll stay." I shrug. Spending the morning with Hayes doesn't sound so bad.

He gets some flour from the kitchen and mixes it in the bucket of water.

"What are you doing?" I ask.

"Good question." Hayes winks. "We're doing papier-mâché today."

While Hayes makes a paste in the kitchen, I help him rip a stack of newspapers into strips. A few other campers join us. I recognize the younger kid who Cassie beat at tetherball our first day of camp. That day feels like a long time ago even though it wasn't.

When I pick up another section of the newspaper and start to rip it up, I notice the date on top of the page. It's late July. Time moves fast here. Or feels fast. Or maybe I just *feel* time here.

"What's black and white and red all over?"

I look up as Grover stands above me. "What?"

"It's a riddle. What's black and white and red all over?" His eyes are hesitant.

"I don't know," I say.

"A newspaper."

"I don't get it."

"Neither do I. I just heard my mom say it once."

"Oh." I push my strips all together on the table, organizing the pile to distract myself from the awkwardness of the moment. I'm sick of it, and while I don't want to go back to the way it was with Grover, I don't want to stay here. "Hayes just told me life isn't about answers, it's about questions, so maybe it doesn't matter if we get it," I offer.

"Maybe." Grover wipes his hair out of his face. "Did you ask him about Maslow and sex?"

I shake my head and look at Grover's lips. He licks them and my stomach jumps. It only makes me more frustrated with him.

"Have you noticed that sometimes Bek doesn't speak English?" Grover asks. I force my eyes off of his lips and on to anything else. "I asked him what he was saying and he told me he has no idea. Apparently, he has a metal plate in his head that picks up frequencies from a French radio station."

"Why do you put up with him?" I ask.

Grover licks his lips again. Damn it. "Why not?"

"But you can't believe a word he says."

"But I can't miss the possibility either."

"The possibility of what?"

"That one day he'll tell the truth. I need to be there for that," Grover says.

"It's worth waiting for," I say and nod.

"Exactly."

Grover and I hold each other's gaze as we stand quiet. I watch him as he watches me. The air is thick with words unspoken, like I could swim through them.

I just need the right question.

"We all have a divine light within us," Hayes says, breaking the moment, his hands in a prayer position at the center of his chest. "But it's our job to seek that divine light and let it shine. To take what's on the inside and show it on the outside. It is the only way to true enlightenment."

As an exercise to help us tap into our inner selves, Hayes tells us that we will be making papier-mâché masks of our own faces.

"You can decorate the outside in any way that you want, but it must represent who you are on the inside."

"Can I be your partner?" Grover asks, when Hayes tells us to pair up. Grover's eyes go back to being hesitant, but it feels like the right question.

"Sure," I say.

Hayes demonstrates how to make papier-mâché. How to dip the newspaper strips in the paste. How to lay them over our partner's face.

"So it doesn't stick, you'll have to add a layer of Vaseline to your skin."

"I knew I'd love this craft," Grover says out loud to the group.

With our supplies gathered, Grover and I find a table and get started.

"Do you want to go first?" Grover holds up a container of Vaseline. But for the first time since I met him, I decide to make a move. I don't need to be tricked into it or forced into it. I jump in on my own accord. I grab the container from Grover.

"You first."

I set out the supplies as Grover sits down in a chair and looks up at me. I think I hear his voice tremble when he says, "I trust you, Zander." And he closes his eyes.

I pop the top open and run my fingers through the gel that feels like thick water. I take a step closer to Grover and look down at the space between us. Our knees are almost touching. Almost. I move in closer so that they do—they touch. His chest rises as he pulls in a breath.

"My dad yells at my mom." Grover's words make me freeze. His eyes stay closed. "She's tried to divorce him five times, but she can never follow through. Last year, he was arrested for public indecency. The cops found him riding his bike around town without any pants on. And the year before that he tried to kill himself. I found him passed out on the bathroom floor."

"Grover," I start to say.

"And I'm scared I'll be just like him. That no matter how hard I look, I'll always be lost." He inhales and pushes more words out. "I'm scared that waiting to die will be my only way of living."

"What do you need from me?" I ask.

The second I say it I know I've found the right question.

"Remind me that I'm not him," Grover says.

I rub my fingers together until they're coated in Vaseline, like thick water that won't come off. My heart pounds in my chest as I move Grover's hair from his forehead with my other hand. When my skin connects with his, shivers run across my arms. I'm electric when I touch him and terrified at the same time. Like I'm breaking open over and over again.

But so is he.

We're breaking open with life.

I feel it.

And Grover needs to feel it, too.

I glance around the room to see if anyone is looking at us, but no one is. I take my time rubbing circles around his forehead even though my cheeks are burning and my fingers tremble. I can't rush this.

The room is so quiet. Grover is so quiet.

I listen to the sound of his breathing.

A whisper in. A whoosh out. Whisper. Whoosh. Whisper. Whoosh.

I move from Grover's forehead to his cheeks. Breathing doesn't always sound this way. Breathing doesn't always sound so natural.

My fingers stroke the bridge of his nose.

Sometimes the only way to breathe is through a machine.

My throat closes tight, but Grover says nothing. He just breathes and he breathes. So I do the same.

For a moment, I pull away. I shake my hands out at my sides and feel the air between my fingers.

Again, *I feel.*

"Are you okay?" Grover finally speaks, his eyes still closed.

I didn't breathe before I got here. That's why my dad cried. That's why I'm here.

"Yes," I say.

I go back to him—to his face and his skin and to the shape of him. I circle my finger over his eyebrows and around the soft spot right under his bottom eyelashes. My fingertips travel down the side of his face to his jaw. They stop there.

His chest rises.

Grover is not his dad. He is alive.

I lean in.

His chest falls.

I lean in closer.

His chest rises.

My hand presses against his cheek now, and still he doesn't open his eyes.

His chest falls.

I lean in so that my lips are inches away from his.

Grover breathes in.

I close my eyes.

He exhales.

I feel his breath on my mouth.

I feel.

I lick my lips and taste the air that's been inside of Grover.

Beautiful breath.

"You are not your dad," I say. I place my hand on Grover's chest. When it lands there, he shudders. For just a moment, he doesn't move. I don't move. I feel his heart beat through the soft cotton of his shirt. And, again, he takes a breath. In and out. In and out. He repeats the simplest—the most instinctual—act of living. Over and over.

He is alive.

The moment I think my hand has stayed too long on him, that if I don't move now I might never let go, Grover puts his hand on top of mine. His voice is soft, nearly a whisper. "I'm so glad you're real."

"And you're alive," I whisper back.

Slowly, he opens his eyes.

"Remind me to write a thank-you note to the makers of Vaseline. Signed every teenage boy."

CHAPTER 21

Dear Mom and Dad,

Have you ever had a Charleston Chew? I'm not sure why they're named Charleston Chew. Maybe they were created in South Carolina? Or the person who invented them was named Charleston, which would be a really weird name, but who am I to judge? My name is Zander.

By the way, why is my name Zander? Did you think I was going to be a boy? You should know Zander isn't really a unisex name. Did you try to make up for it when you picked Molly's name? Hers is so girly.

Did you notice what I did right there? Hers is so girly. Present tense. See. Molly can still be present tense even though she's dead. "Molly is dead" is present tense. And you spent so many years worrying about her being past tense.

The only issue with Charleston Chews is that the chocolate sticks to your teeth and gets caught in the crevasses. Please make me a dentist appointment for when I get home.

Z

We stand around a lit campfire as Kerry leads us in our fifth James Taylor song for the evening and Hayes plays the guitar. "You've Got a Friend" has never sounded worse.

Cassie sits next to me and whispers, "So you're in, right?"

I nod. As if I could ever be out. I can't leave her now and I don't want to.

When the sing-along is over and we've abused James Taylor's entire collection of sappy ballads, Kerry gathers the entire camp around him.

"Tonight is Black Out Night. Every light at camp will be turned off. The fire extinguished. Every sound silent. There will be no talking."

Hayes and a junior counselor named Shiloh dump a pile of sand on top of the lit bonfire, and it sizzles to nothing.

"The only guides you will have as we find our way home are the stars in the sky and the light in your soul. But that's okay. *Trust* yourself. You may be lost, but *trus*t that you know where you're going. *Trust* that you can find yourself even in the darkness."

I look up at the sky and then at Cassie in the dark. She gags herself.

"The counselors will lead you blindfolded to the fence that lines the property of camp. It is your job to find your way back to us." Campers start looking from one person to the next. Even I get a bit nervous. I've seen a good portion of camp, but nowhere near all of it. The property is expansive. Cassie, on the other hand, just yawns exaggeratedly. "Don't worry," Kerry says through the tension. "Each of you will be given a whistle. If you fear you're lost, blow the whistle and a counselor will come and find you. You have one hour to make it back. Then the lights will come back on, and we will meet in the Circle of Hope. Your reward for completing the task?" Kerry smiles. "S'mores."

"Some reward," Cassie whispers. "A fat-sicle made out of marshmallow. Why doesn't Kerry just give us diabetes?"

The counselors line us up single file, handing out whistles, and blindfolding each camper, placing our hands on the person in front of us. When the entire camp is ready, Kerry says, "We pray to Saint

Anthony that the lost be found. That the soul be free. That life be everlasting."

And we start walking.

I hold on tight to Cassie in front of me. She walks at a steady pace. At one point the line slows down and I run into her back. Her hair smells like the lake. I saw her practicing her kicking today when I left arts and crafts. She took off her life jacket to float on her own in the red zone and a junior counselor blew a loud whistle and made her put it back on. Cassie looked annoyed, but I could see satisfaction on her face.

I smell her hair again as I step behind her.

"When they break us up, just stay put. I'll find you," Cassie whispers to me in the dark.

My mom would have a stroke if she knew I was out in the woods alone with no way of getting back. And didn't Madison say there are bears here? I grip tighter on Cassie's shoulders.

"Relax, Z."

The line comes to a stop and someone detaches my hands from Cassie's shoulders. For a moment, I stand in the dark like a buoy out at sea just waiting for a wave to hit it and make it move. When I'm about to take off my blindfold, someone grabs my hands and leads me away.

"I've got you, Zander," Madison's voice is in my ear. She places my hand on something cold. "Count back from one hundred and then remove your blindfold."

I hear footsteps backing away from me and then it's quiet. I start counting in my head, but my hand stays put. I don't let go of what I'm touching. I used to like disappearing into my head, but now with every number my heart pulses harder. I couldn't disappear if I wanted to. I'd miss living too much.

When I get to one, I rip the blindfold off. I'm standing at the fence that lines Camp Padua—the fence that separates the world and me. The air is silent. I spin in a circle looking for anyone, but all I see are trees and all I smell is pine. I miss Cassie's hair.

But she said she'd find me.

I run my hand along the cold metal boundary. Everything I left is on the other side—people and stores and school and Molly's empty room. But what I want is Cassie.

An empty feeling comes over me. I don't want to go to the other side of the fence. Madison is right. I'm not lost here at camp. But out there . . . I step away from the boundary.

My eyes search for Cassie in the darkness. When something buzzes in my ear, I don't bother swatting it away. It will be back. They always come back. I'm even used to the mosquitoes now. I'll miss them when I'm home. I'll miss so much.

Cassie comes out of the darkness then, like a light sent to save me from disappearing down a black hole.

"Come on." She grins at me. "We need to get down to the lake."

The farther away from the fence we get, the better I feel. We walk quietly for a while. I just listen to the familiar sounds of camp.

"How did you know this was going to happen?" I ask.

"It happens every year," Cassie says.

"How many years have you been coming here?"

Cassie shrugs and looks off, avoiding eye contact. "I don't know. Too many."

"Well, how did you know where to find me?"

"I didn't. I just knew I'd find you eventually."

"I'm glad you did," I say.

Cassie makes a face like my compliment is more like a torture device. I mimic it back at her.

The equipment shed on the beach is closed, but not locked. Cassie pulls the doors open to reveal Grover and Bek sitting on the floor in complete darkness.

"Sorry to interrupt, boys." Cassie walks in and pulls on the dangling string that turns on the shed's dull light.

"Bek and I were just playing the silent game," Grover says.

"You lose." Bek points at Grover.

"I can't stay silent any longer. It's too difficult to hold things in. Don't you think, Zander?" Grover grabs my hand and pulls me down next to him.

"We don't have time for one of your weird, psychological conversations where everything means something else, Cleve." Cassie closes the shed doors and begins to dig around the equipment.

"Am I that obvious?"

"Yes," the whole group says in unison.

Grover sits back, looking slightly deflated. His hand is inches from mine. Subtly, I move over until the tips of our fingers are touching and his smile comes back.

Cassie pulls the duffel bag out from behind the life jackets, her face beaming. We all sit in a small circle staring at her, like she just found gold. Or drugs. Or a secret stash of beer.

"Jackpot," she says, unzipping the bag. She places it down in the center of the circle. My stomach does flips as we all lean in to see what's in the bag.

Uncontrollable giggles erupt out of me as I reach into the bag and pull a piece of its contents free.

"Candy?" I snicker like a little kid. "You stole candy?"

"Yeah, so what?" Cassie says. "The camp nurse is orca fat, like she needs any more candy. I was doing her a favor by stealing her stash."

"I thought it was pills or booze, but candy? It's just so . . ."

"So what?"

"So . . . innocent."

I get up and hug Cassie. She pushes me back.

"Jesus, Z, calm down."

"I'm just so relieved." I sit back down next to Grover.

"Relieved that I'm not crazy?"

"Oh no," I say unwrapping a pack of Skittles. "You're crazy. You're just not as crazy as I thought."

Cassie grabs a box of Nerds. "Thanks, Z."

We sit, eating the candy out of Cassie's duffel bag, all of us quiet for a while. Bek downs two chocolate bars in record time. Cassie grimaces at him, and he flashes her a chocolate-coated-teeth smile. Grover laughs as he pops M&M'S in his mouth one at a time.

I move from Skittles to chocolate to Airheads. There's so much candy. It's like Halloween in summer. It sticks in my teeth and on the roof of my mouth. The sugar hits my system like adrenaline bombs. I feel giddy and high, but an innocent high, like riding a bike too fast down a hill. I know I might crash, but the wind on my face makes me feel invincible. It's like I'm making up for every time my mom served me a fruit smoothie with kale instead of ice cream. She used to say that fruit tastes better than artificial sugar anyway. That's total bullshit. Artificial sweeteners are amazing.

"Why do parents lie to us?" I say with a mouthful of unnatural-blue Airheads.

"To protect us I think," Grover says.

"From what?" I ask.

"Life. I guess," he says.

"But if we're protected from our own lives then are we *really* living?"

"You sound like Grover, Z." Cassie rolls her eyes.

"I mean it." I sit up straight. My head spins a little bit, the candy high taking over. "I don't want to be protected anymore. If I want to eat high-fructose corn syrup, I want to eat it."

"Say it, sister." Bek gives me a fist pump with his chubby hand.

"Just prepare to get fat." Cassie shakes her head.

"At least it would be *my* choice to get fat. My parents never ask me anything. I mean, I take French because my dad told me I had to take it." My hands start to shake at my side. Like the sugar has overloaded my system, I start talking without thinking. "They didn't ask me how I felt about Molly either. They didn't ask if I wanted my practically dead sister living in my house for six years. Six years! They just moved her down the hallway from me and made me love her. They made me love her. But my parents were lying. They knew she was dead the whole time. They knew it!"

"Zander." Grover grabs one of my shaking hands, forcing my eyes to come into focus. Bek and Cassie stare at me. My chin falls to my chest and, again, I let go.

"She choked on an apple," I say. "Molly choked on an apple when she was two." I let the words I've said sit around me. "Our neighbor down the street used to watch Molly when my mom and dad were at work and I was at school. Mrs. Moore was her name. She was really nice. Every day when my mom and I picked Molly up, she'd give me a sucker. Those little ones that come in all different flavors like root beer and coconut that cashiers at the grocery store give out to kids." I take a breath, practically able to taste one. "Mrs. Moore was in the kitchen doing the dishes or something after Molly had eaten lunch and Molly was in the living room playing. When Mrs. Moore went to check on her she found Molly passed out on the floor, a slice of apple in her hand. Molly had suffocated. When they got to the hospital, she was put on life support. There were so many machines and sounds and she was just lying there like she might wake up. Like she was asleep."

I suck in a breath and hold it inside of me. Beautiful, real breath. Then I exhale the rest out.

"My parents couldn't let go of her, even though the doctors tried to reason with them. They said it was unlikely she would ever wake up, but my parents wouldn't listen. They insisted on bringing her home. They filled her room with machines—everything she needed to stay alive. But she wasn't living. She wasn't running or jumping or talking. She was just lying there, breathing because a machine said she could. And the worst part is that I got used to it. I got used to seeing her and talking to her. I watched her grow and get long. And then one day it all ended. Molly's body gave out. Just like the doctors said—she never woke up. By then Mrs. Moore had moved away. I heard my neighbor say that she couldn't stand seeing our house, knowing what was inside and what she had done, so she moved back to California. And now all that's left in Molly's room is silence."

The shed stays quiet for a moment, and then Grover says, "That's why you don't eat apples."

"My parents never asked me what I wanted. My mom quit her job to take care of Molly. She changed our whole lives so that we lived in a bubble. A bubble made of healthy food and good choices and hovering parents who made sure I never made a mistake." I stop and correct myself. "Almost never. But bubbles burst and people die no matter how hard we try to stay alive."

"What mistake did you make?" Bek asks.

I look at him and then Cassie. It's time for me to fulfill my promise to her. "I almost drowned at a swim meet."

"What?" she screams.

"I didn't want to tell you."

"God, Z, I trusted you."

I start to talk fast now, fidgeting with my hands. Grover said it's hard to stay silent. It's hard to hold things in. People can drown in silence just as easily as drowning in a pool.

"My parents made me sign up for swim team after Molly died," I say, words spilling from my mouth. "They thought it would help me 'get back out there.' That's what my dad said. 'Get back out there.' But I didn't want to be out there. I wanted noise in my house again. I hate silence. But I did it. I went to every practice and every meet. I lived with the smell of chlorine on my skin and my coach's bad breath. I became a machine. A living and breathing machine. Just like Molly. I felt nothing. I moved when people told me to. I ate when my mom told me to. I kissed Coop when he told me to. I swam when my coach told me to. And then one day I was in the middle of a relay race and I was winning. I could see the girls beside me through the water. They were trying so hard to beat me. And I didn't care. I didn't care if I won. I didn't care if I lost. I didn't care. So I stopped. Right there in the middle of the pool. I stopped moving. I stopped breathing. And I let myself sink to the bottom."

"What happened?" Grover asks.

"I woke up on the side of the pool, my coach's mouth on top of mine."

"Coach Garlic Breath?" Cassie asks. "Oh my God, that's disgusting."

"My dad signed me up for camp the next day." I fold my arms in my lap. "That's why I'm here."

No one says anything for a moment. When Grover puts his hand on my back, I don't pull away. I'm done pulling away.

"Voici mon secret," Bek says, surprising me. We all turn to look at him.

"Uh-oh, the French radio station must be coming through." Grover knocks Bek on the side of the head. "Is that better, bud?"

"Here is my secret," I repeat what Bek said in English.

"It's from *The Little Prince*. My mom always read the French version because she was from Quebec."

"Wait." Grover tries to make eye contact with Bek, but he doesn't look up. "You said your mom *was* from Quebec."

"Yeah. She's kind of dead."

Cassie, Grover, and I look at each other, unsure if Bek is actually telling the truth. The corners of his mouth pull down into the deepest frown I have ever seen. The kind of frown your face makes when you're about to cry and you can't control it, like your emotions are forcing their way to the surface and they won't be denied.

"She read it to me every night before bed. I share a room with two of my younger brothers, but she always took time just to acknowledge me."

"How many siblings do you have?" I ask.

"Six. She was busy, but I always knew she noticed me when she read that book." Bek picks up another piece of candy and unwraps it. "My dad doesn't really do that. He's kind of sad all the time now because she's gone and he works a lot . . . and he's kind of an ass. So now, no one notices me."

"So you lie to get noticed," Grover says.

Bek puts the Jolly Rancher in his mouth. He doesn't say yes or no. Cassie eyes him up and down like she's seeing him for the first time.

"Well, since we're confessing things, I guess I should tell you guys that I sign myself up for camp every year," Grover says.

"What do your parents say?" Bek asks.

Grover looks at Bek and shrugs. "It's better than playing on a baseball league all summer."

And then out of the sadness and reality that's circling around us, laughter begins to bubble up in me. "I can't believe you sign yourself up."

Bek's frown starts to lighten. He snickers.

"Baseball *would* require running," Bek says.

"Now, that's the truth," Grover says.

"I'm too fat to run."

"Another truth!" Grover points at him, his face bright. "I think Bek is cured. Is your name really Alex Trebek?"

"Yes."

"Man." Grover rubs his chin. "Now I think he's lying again." Bek's shoulders start to bounce. Mine mimic his, as my head gets light and fuzzy. "Answer: A psychological disorder categorized by the compulsive or pathological behavior of a person toward lying," Grover says.

I raise my hand. "What is compulsive liar?"

"Correct!" Grover points at me.

"I'll take dead sisters for one thousand, Alex," I say.

Bek snickers hard through his teeth as his stomach jiggles. "But I really am Alex Trebek."

"No, I really am Alex Trebek." Grover points at himself.

"No," I say. "You're Grover Cleveland."

He nods. "I *am* Grover Cleveland."

Suddenly our giggles move into a full-blown fit of hysterics. I clutch my stomach because it hurts from laughing and eating and letting all my secrets out. But I feel better, even in this musty equipment shed.

It's all finally out. The weight that pulled me down to the bottom of the pool is gone. I'm lighter. I gasp in tiny breaths, as my eyes water over with tears that spill down my face. This is what it feels like to cry happy tears. In this damp, humid place, the sun is back.

Cassie stands up from the circle and starts clapping, slow and steady. We all stop and look at her. The only sound in the shed is her skin smacking together. Cassie's straight face has washed away and anger sits there now. I swallow down my giggles and wipe clean the tears from my cheeks. Her eyes narrow on all of us.

"Well, isn't it just so funny how sad you all are with your sad stories." Her voice is strained. I can see the muscles tighten on her neck. "Poor Bek and his dead mom. Poor Zander and her dead sister."

"Cassie." Grover attempts to touch her arm, but she yanks it away. She's shaking. Her eyes burn in the dull light of the equipment shed.

"At least you have a family to be sad about." Her words smack me in the face. No one moves. Cassie grabs the duffel bag off the ground and throws the shed door open. Before any of us can call her back, she's gone.

CHAPTER 22

Dear Mom and President Cleveland,
I have found my first lady.
Your son,
Grover Cleveland

Bek runs after Cassie. He's out of the shed before Grover or I can say a word. I watch his round silhouette bounding over the sand and up the stairs toward the mess hall.

"I think Bek is in love with Cassie," Grover says, sitting back on his hands.

"Should we follow her?" I start to get up, but he holds me still with his hand on my leg.

"She needs to cool off."

I look down at his hand, resting on my skin, and nod.

Candy wrappers lie all around us. I collect them all into a pile, like a sugar junkyard.

"So Molly . . ." Grover says.

I organize the plastic wrappers, unable to look him in the eye. "Now you know why I said I don't know anything about her. I mean, she was two when it all happened. I didn't get the chance to know her."

"You know her, Zander." When Grover says that, I look at him. "You just know her for what her life was. Sometimes that's all we get."

"She didn't have a life."

"Maybe not the way we think of life, but it was a life nonetheless." Grover pauses. "Kind of like my dad."

"Molly deserved better."

"So does he."

"I'm sorry," I say.

Grover scoots closer to me and says, "Maybe we can either be mad at what we don't know or deal with what we do know. And you *don't* know what her life would have looked like. Molly could have turned into a heroin addict or . . ." Grover puts his fist into his mouth and bites down onto it. "Joined a sorority in college."

Grover's other hand hasn't left my leg. It's warm.

"She never would have joined a sorority." One of my cheeks pulls into a smile.

"Fine, she could have been homecoming queen."

"Well, now you've taken it too far." I smile fully. My eyes rest on Grover's hand. "What about you?" I ask.

"The chair will eventually break." Grover's finger circles my skin. "To exist means knowing that one day you won't, right?"

"But that doesn't mean we stop living," I say. I try to melt the lump that forms in my throat, swallowing over and over, as I look at him. But it stays. I don't want anything to happen to him. I want Grover to stay exactly like he is. I want to hold his chair together until my hands bleed.

"Where do you live?" I ask.

Grover smiles but doesn't look up. "Less than five miles away. You can see my house from the H dock."

"What?"

"I remember when Kerry opened the camp. I was six. My mom read about it in the paper. Since she can't really leave my dad, it just kind of fits that I do something local." Grover looks up at the dull light hanging from the top of the shed. "I like to think that I was meant for this place. It makes me feel better about . . . everything."

"Can I see where you live?" I ask.

Before Grover can make it go away, I see sadness sitting on his face. I see a little boy with broken parents living in a broken house who just wants to meet people who are broken, too, so it doesn't hurt so badly. And then it's gone and my Grover is back.

We walk to the end of the H dock. The lights are still out at camp, but around the lake, houses are lit up. I forgot that people vacation on Lake Kimball, and people live here. I've blocked them out, like I've blocked out everything else beyond the border of this place. As Grover stands behind me, I can feel his chest inches from my back. He leans down, resting his head on my shoulder, and points off to the right.

"See the house with the blinking red light?" Grover whispers in my ear.

I search all the lights until I find it on the other side of the lake.

"I do," I say, happy. I see him now.

I turn to face Grover, my nose almost touching his shirt. My head barely reaches the top of his chest. I breathe him in as my eyes drift up from his shirt to his collarbone to his neck and finally rest on his lips. They're round and moist and painted a few different colors from all of the candy we ate. Sugar is still on them probably. I lick my own lips.

"Don't leave," Grover says.

"What?"

"Don't leave. I'll be right back."

He runs off the dock, shaking it with every step and leaving me alone. I want him back by my side the moment he's gone. I wrap my arms around my body as my stomach twists in tight knots, and the breeze on the water picks up. Grover was blocking me from the cold. I don't like being here without him.

But he's back before my worry gets out of control. He huffs and puffs across the dock until he's standing right in front of me. He takes a step closer. My nose is inches away from the center of his chest, from his heart. The wind stops. Time stops. Life pauses so I can take this moment in. He exhales a tired breath as I look up at his face and finally let out the air I'd been holding in to keep everything inside of me steady.

"I had to get something to eat," he says.

"Of course." I start to roll my eyes, but what he has in his hand stops me. He holds up the red, shiny object. Grover takes a bite of the apple. I watch his lips curve around it with ease. "Watch out. There's poison in there," I say.

"It's worth the risk," he counters with a mouthful of apple.

I bite the side of my lip as I wonder what the inside of Grover's mouth tastes like. I'm jealous of the apple.

A drop of apple juice sits on the center of his lips, like a tiny bubble of sweetness. I gnaw on the inside of my cheek. Forget candy, I want that drop. I want it like I want breath. Grover takes another bite and a pinhead of juice lands on my bare shoulder. I wipe my finger over it and put it to my mouth. It tastes more like sunscreen than apple juice. It's not good enough. *This* is not good enough. And Grover makes it look so easy. The way his lips curve and press and gnaw at the apple. I gasp in a weightless breath as the bottom of my stomach gets tight. I don't know what I want more—Grover or the apple. Or both. I want them both. I want to feel both, and I know I won't be satisfied with life if I don't have them. I will always be lost. And Molly will always be dead. And I will always be one moment from sinking, one moment from shattering, one moment from really living. Glass can break, but that doesn't mean it's weak. Sometimes the shards are all we get.

I look into Grover's eyes and tilt my chin toward his mouth. "I acknowledge the poison. But life is worth it."

"Amen." Grover leans in close to my face. He smells sugary. I place my hands on his chest and feel his heart beat. He is alive and I am alive.

"Let me taste it," I say.

Grover pulls my chin toward his. I suck in his sweet breath.

And his lips connect with mine.

They're warm and soft, and for now, they're all for me. The taste of apple swirls from Grover's mouth into mine as our lips part and our tongues meet. Sweetness floods me. His sweetness, the apple's, mine, they tangle together. If there is poison in this, I'll risk it. I will risk a life with poison to have this moment forever.

I lean into Grover, my hands moving from his chest to his neck. I pull him closer to me. I run my tongue over his lips, grabbing every speck of flavor I can. Like I've been starved my whole life and I'm just realizing it. And now I can't stop wanting more of everything.

Grover's hands come up to my shoulders. He gently pushes me away. When air touches the spot where Grover's lips just were, I'm disappointed.

He stammers, "I . . . I'm worried my heightened mental and emotional state won't recover from this moment. I might explode if kept like this too long." I feel my cheeks heat. I look down at Grover's shorts. He grabs my chin and shakes his head. "For once I'm not talking about that," he says.

"That's a relief." I smile.

"If I did explode, would you put me back together?"

I take the apple from Grover's hand and inspect it. It's not without fault. A brown bruise sits on the skin.

"I prefer you broken." I bite into the bruise on the apple and swallow it down. Then I toss it into Lake Kimball. It doesn't sink and I can't help but giggle.

Apples float.

Grover and I make it back to the Circle of Hope just as Kerry gathers all the campers around him. Grover squeezes my hand one time before letting me go.

Madison exhales a dramatic breath. "You made it back."

"I did."

"And everything's all right?" she asks.

"No." I smile. "Everything will never be all right. But maybe that's the point."

Madison smiles and nods. "Maybe."

Just then, Cassie sidles up next to me.

"Blah, blah, blah, she's fine, Mads. Go take a Xanax." Cassie pulls me away, her nails digging into my arms. "Aren't you going to ask me if *I'm* okay?"

"No. I know you're not okay," I say.

"It doesn't matter anymore," Cassie says.

"Why not?" I ask. Cassie starts pacing in front of me, her eyes focused hard on the ground. I watch her closely. "Cassie, what is it?"

"I'm sick of being red. I want yellow."

"What?"

"Didn't you hear me?" Cassie gets in my face. Her eyes lock on mine. "I'm sick of being red. I want yellow. I need to retake my swim test."

My worry melts away as a large smile pulls my cheeks high on my face. I touch my lips and remember how Grover felt.

"Yes," I say. "You do."

CHAPTER 23

Chère Cassie,

Je t'aime.

Cordialement,

Alex Trebek

At breakfast the next morning, Cassie tells Madison that she wants a retest. She even follows all the rules of her punishment, sitting at the counselors' table without any dramatics or arguments.

"Please," Cassie asks, a fake wide grin on her face, and Madison agrees.

I go through the line, grabbing an extra piece of toast, and bring it over to Cassie.

"Are you trying to make me look like Bek?" she asks.

"Eat it. You need it."

Cassie groans. "It better not have butter on it."

"Trust me. I know you better than you think."

She narrows her eyes and wipes her finger across the dry bread.

I shrug at her before walking away, then watch her from across the mess hall to make sure she takes at least a few bites. She does. She doesn't eat the whole thing, but she eats some, which is better than where she started.

After breakfast, I stay in the mess hall to decorate our papier-mâché masks. Hayes sets out paint and gives us what he calls an "intention" for the activity.

"Let the world know who you are today. For today is all we have. Yesterday is gone and tomorrow may never happen."

Grover puts his finger up in the air. "Technically, this moment is all we have if you really think about it. And then it's gone. Isn't it weird that everything that's coming out of my mouth is going directly into the past? Like just a few seconds ago when I said, 'technically this moment is all we have.' That is a memory now. And that is a memory now. And that is a memory now."

"Yes." Hayes seems to falter in his evenness.

Grover points at him. "You saying that is now a memory! So what you really want us to do is paint who we are presently, knowing that it will be who we were in the past the second it's actually there."

"Yes." Hayes drags out the word like he's not sure what is really going on. I nudge Grover in the side.

"Got it. Geez. I'm gonna need to think about this."

"I think you think too much," Hayes says.

"I think you're probably right about me thinking too much. But if all of life turns into a memory the moment after it happens, all we really have are our thoughts. And mine have a possible impending expiration date, so I better use them while I can. Don't you think?"

"Sure." Hayes now looks totally confused. Satisfaction spreads on Grover's face. "Let's get started."

"Let's make some memories!" Grover yells.

But I'm too distracted thinking about Cassie and Grover's lips and the fact that who we are at this moment is not who we will be. I don't want to waste time wondering who I am. I just want to be.

When Hayes asks us all to show our completed masks to the group, mine is blank.

"Interesting choice, Durga, and quite poetic," he says.

"Genius," Grover counters. His mask is a replica of Abraham Lincoln, top hat and all. "No one knows what Grover Cleveland looks like, so I went with the popular president, but you get it."

"I just figured why waste time looking at who I was in the past," I say.

"Amen." Grover smiles.

At the end of the activity, Grover and I leave our masks behind. Those people don't exist anymore.

Cassie and I stand on the beach waiting for her to retake her swim test. A few counselors watch as well. I'm pretty sure half of them hope she'll drown. She squeezes her hands at her sides and shakes out her arms.

"Just pretend I'm holding you."

"God, you're such a lesbian." I cock my head at Cassie. "Sorry. That just slipped out."

"Did you eat?" I ask.

"Of course I ate."

"You say that like it's a given."

"Nothing in life is a given," Cassie says.

"Did you eat?" I ask again.

"A little. I didn't feel well."

"You're nervous. That's okay."

"Sticks!" Grover runs down the steps from the mess hall. A smile grows on Cassie's face the second she sees him. "Maslow wanted me to give these to you."

"Fucking Maslow, again?" she snaps.

Grover looks at me. We both shrug at the same time.

Cassie takes a swig from the box of Lemonheads and hands it to me. "If I die it's your fault."

"Stop being dramatic."

"Stop being . . ." Cassie narrows her eyes on me. "Just shut up."

No snarky remark. She must be really nervous.

Grover and I walk Cassie down to the water. Madison stands in front of the At Camp Padua There's FUN in FUNdamentals board with a clipboard and a stopwatch in her hand, talking to another counselor. Cassie's red washer sits on the board like a target.

"You can do this," I say and squeeze Cassie's hand.

"Zander's right," Grover adds.

"Oh, shut the fuck up. What is this? Group share-apy?" Cassie shakes her hands loose.

Grover smiles. "That's my girl."

When Cassie's standing in the water and Madison is about to start the test, a screaming voice makes everyone freeze.

"Wait!" Bek's bright red face appears at the top of the steps. He fumbles his way down, carrying a bow and arrow set from the archery field. Judging by his heavy breathing, he must have run the whole way. "Wait!"

Bek almost slips on his face in the sand as he sprints up to Cassie. He drops the bow and arrow on the beach and runs straight into the water, shoes and all. He grabs her by the arms.

"What the hell, Baby Fat? Get your sweaty paws off of me."

But Bek doesn't listen to Cassie. Before anyone has a moment of warning, he plants his lips on top of Cassie's and kisses her. She freezes, Bek's chubby fingers holding on to her skinny arms. Grover and I gasp at the same time along with everyone else watching.

When he finally pulls back, Bek still doesn't let go. Cassie stands, her two feet like cement blocks unable to move.

"All right, Bek!" Grover yells and claps loudly. He puts his two fingers in his mouth and blows a loud whistle. The sound must shock

Cassie out of her trance because she finally shakes free from Bek and takes a step back. She winds up her arm and smacks his face.

"Get away from me, Porky," she snaps.

He falls back in the water, but catches himself before toppling over. As he walks out of Lake Kimball, his hand on his red cheek, a wide smile sits on his face.

"Je t'aime," he whispers as he walks past Grover and me in a haze and heads back up the steps without another word.

I turn to Grover. "What the hell just happened?"

"I think Bek finally hit his target." He smirks. I study the slope of Grover's nose and the way the end curves slightly off to the right. I think I know the feeling. At this moment, I'm so thankful for imperfections.

"I think I want to take Spanish next year instead of French," I whisper to him.

"Wise choice, señorita."

Madison explains that Cassie must first swim between the docks twice in any stroke that she chooses to prove that she can swim at least one of them.

"It doesn't have to be good," Cassie clarifies.

"No," Madison says. "Just don't put your feet down." And for a moment, Madison examines Cassie with a genuine look of affection and says, "You can do this."

"Whatever, J.Crew," Cassie scoffs, ignoring the moment.

When that's done, she must go to the deep side of the H dock and tread for five minutes.

Cassie walks out farther into the water and dips her body down. She covers herself to her shoulders, surrounded by what she was so afraid of just a little while ago. It's one of the most beautiful things I've ever seen, like when the sun comes up in the desert and coats the sky like a healing blanket. But my whole body gets tight when Madison blows her whistle, even my breathing.

"It's just me, Mads. You don't need to be so fucking formal." Cassie flicks water at her, getting Madison's legs and shorts wet.

"Let's do this," Madison says.

Grover grabs my hand and I squeeze back.

"Trust yourself!" I yell to Cassie. She looks back at us. I nod and smile at her.

Grover clutches my hand tighter. At the same time, we start to repeat, "We pray to Saint Anthony that the lost be found. That the soul be free. That life be everlasting."

When Cassie walks out of the water after the test, she picks up the arrow Bek dropped on the sand and walks over to the board where her red washer hangs. Cassie slams the arrow right through the center.

Bull's-eye.

COURAGE

CHAPTER 24

Dear Mom and Dad,

How are you? How are you really? I keep getting letters about what you're doing (podcast club still sounds awful by the way), but I can't tell how you feel. We talk a lot about how we feel here at Camp Padua. My friend, Dori, hates her stepdad. This other girl in my cabin, Hannah, cuts herself because she hates herself. She hasn't come out and said it, but I think she will. At least that's what Cassie says. Cassie is my friend here. She literally hates everything in the world, except maybe Grover. Some days I think she doesn't hate me, too. But then others I think she needs to hate me because it makes her feel better when I don't give up on her. And that makes me feel good.

I taught her how to swim, too.

I guess what I'm saying is that I hope when I come home we can talk about how we feel. I hope . . .

After the swim meet when I almost drowned, I know why Dad almost hit me. And it's okay. Don't worry. It won't happen again.

I'm not sinking anymore.

Z

PS—Grover is a boy here and he's delightful. Mom, you can tell Cooper I said that the next time you see him in the grocery store.

Cassie moves back into our cabin at the end of the week, after her "solitary" confinement. She bursts through the door.

"I'm back," she announces in a singsong tone. She walks over to her bed, drops her duffel bag, and picks up the quilt I left there.

"What the hell is this?"

"It was Molly's."

"Gross." She tosses it back down on her bed. "You put your dead sister's quilt on my bed?"

"I thought you might need it, jerk."

When I go to take it back, Cassie stops me. "Jerk?"

"It was the first thing that popped into my head."

"We need to work on your insults, Z."

And then Cassie spreads the quilt out on her bed. When she goes into the bathroom to brush her teeth, I take a peek inside the duffel bag. The candy is gone. I unzip the pouch that housed all her diet pills on the first day of camp. They're still there. She's kept her promise. I put it back exactly how it was.

When Cassie walks out of the bathroom, I can't help but smile at her.

"What the hell are you staring at, jerk?" she asks me.

I'm glad she's back. I've missed her.

❦

The Circle of Hope is quiet. My eyes focus down at the task at hand. I pull the plastic gimp string tight and then start over with the pattern, crisscrossing the colors and looping the opposite string through the holes. Everyone is hard at work except for Cassie, who's lying in the grass popping heads off of dandelions. She's surrounded in a graveyard of broken weeds.

The object of the lesson is simple, so Madison says. Make a colorful key chain out of gimp and present it to a person with a confession about yourself. That person will then carry around a reminder of the courage it takes to be honest about who you are and thus be reminded of the courage inside all of us.

"We need courage to get through the hard times in life," Madison says as she walks around the group. "When we're feeling down, when we're nervous we might fail, when it seems like everything and everyone is against us, we need courage to get back on our feet and start again."

I twist orange, yellow, and pink gimp one over another, repeating the pattern to make the key chain. When our group share-apy time is almost up, Madison comes around with a lighter to burn the end of the gimp so the plastic melts together.

Hannah walks up to me and holds out her key chain. "For you."

I try not to look startled, though I'm pretty sure I do a bad job of it.

"Thank you," I say hesitantly.

"Girls make fun of me," she blurts out. "The girls at my school. Ever since I was in kindergarten. I don't know why, but they do, so I figure something must be wrong with me, right? Something *must* be wrong with me for them to hate me so much."

"I don't know. Maybe they just suck."

"Maybe." Hannah squints her eyes like she's thinking hard.

"Is that why you cut yourself?"

She looks down at her long-sleeved shirt. "I can see it then. I can see what's wrong with me because it's on my skin." I nod slowly, an ache in my stomach for her. I take the key chain from Hannah. "Also, I think I might be in love with Kerry," she says.

"Kerry? Like owner of the camp, Kerry?"

Hannah nods. "He's gorgeous."

"He's also twice your age."

"I know." Hannah gets a pensive look on her face. She fidgets with her hands. "Also, I was the one who shut the window."

"What?"

"I shut the window when Cassie snuck out. Please don't tell her I did it. She might kill me."

Hannah's right. Cassie might kill her. I hold up the key chain. It must have taken some courage for Hannah to shut the window. Courage or insanity. "I won't say anything."

Hannah looks relieved of her confession as she walks away. I find Cassie still in the field and sit down next to her.

"Mama had a baby and her head popped off." Cassie squeezes the dandelion where the stem meets the flower. The yellow head disconnects and flies through the air, landing next to my leg.

I hold out my key chain. "Here."

Cassie sits up and takes it. "Aren't you supposed to confess something?"

"I told you everything a few nights ago."

"That's impossible. You couldn't have told me *everything*."

I hug my arms around my chest. "Grover kissed me."

Cassie's back gets straight and she looks down at the key chain. "Is he a good kisser?" Her voice sounds tight and I wish I could take the words back, but I can't, so I'm honest.

"He is."

Cassie stands up and dusts off the back of her shorts but doesn't look at me. Her eyes focus hard on something invisible across the fire pit. "Bek isn't a bad kisser either . . . if you get past the fat rolls. And I don't really give a shit what you and Grover do. You can have his babies for all I care. But I highly recommend you think about that because you two are bound to have insane children." She looks down at all of the decapitated dandelions.

I pull one from the grass and offer it to her. Maybe she needs to break something. She takes it and finally looks at me. "Just remember who introduced you. I was friends with him first."

"I could never forget."

We spend the rest of the afternoon swimming between the shallow and deep end of the H dock with Bek and Grover. When we get down to the beach, Cassie slams Bek against the wooden board and tells him if his lips ever come close to hers again, she'll cut off his balls.

"If I can even find them," she snaps, her hands pressing into his chest to hold him still.

Bek just smiles widely. "You're touching me."

"Another truth. Seriously, I think Bek is cured," Grover says.

Cassie grunts, like she's totally disgusted, and lets him go. She takes her new yellow washer and hangs it up, like a ray of sunlight, on the board.

She asks me to show her how to do more than a lame-looking freestyle stroke, and I spend the afternoon teaching her how to tilt her head and breathe as she swims. And then we work on breaststroke.

"My favorite stroke," Grover pipes up. "Don't think I didn't notice the new suit." He eyes my two-piece.

"Did someone say *breast*?" Bek's head bobs above the water. "And *stroke*?"

After Cassie's mini-lesson, Grover and I swim out to the raft and dive off, seeing who can touch the bottom and come back up the quickest with a handful of sand. Cassie watches us as she holds on to the end of the H dock, unable to swim out farther than the buoys that mark the line between yellow and green.

I dive deep into the water and push as fast as I can. When I touch the bottom, I grab sand. I turn fast and slam my feet into the ground to propel myself toward the surface, leaving behind, at the bottom of Lake Kimball, the memory of how easy it was for me to slip under.

"Who came up first?" Grover yells, spitting water out of his mouth.

"I did." I splash him, still holding my handful of sand.

"Cassie's the judge." He points at her while treading water, his arm up.

Cassie seems to examine our raised handfuls of sand, and she says, "Cleve did."

I push him, smudging my sand on his arm. It drips into the water and dissipates. "She's a biased judge."

Grover smiles and comes after me. He pulls on my legs, dragging me closer to him, and under the surface of the water. He wrestles me around as I squirm, my laughs forming bubbles all around my head. We come up gasping for air at the same time.

He smiles at me.

And I smile at him.

We both duck back under the surface. I sink just enough so that my head is less than a foot away from the top. The sun glistens through the greenish-blue water as Grover moves toward me so that his face is inches from mine. My hair floats around me. He runs his fingers through it, making it wave like grass in the wind. I do the same.

Then we kiss for a second time. His lips lightly press to mine, and we just stay there, floating just below the surface.

When the boys go up to shower for dinner, Cassie and I sit on the end of the dock, our hair still wet and our faces upturned toward the sun.

"Before my sister was born, my mom used to take a few days off of work every summer so she could take me to the pool. She'd buy me one of those red, white, and blue popsicles from the snack stand."

"Those are packed with high-fructose corn syrup."

"I know. I can't believe my mom let me have it." I smile at the memory I'd forgotten until now. "The car would get so hot sitting in the sun, but it felt so good at the end of the day."

"My mom did nothing for me." Cassie skims her feet across the water.

"That can't be true. She had to do something."

"Other than give me lice?" She looks down at her wrinkled hands. I give Cassie a few seconds and a few more. "She did one thing I guess. She taught me how to braid. Every black girl needs to know how to braid hair."

"Will you braid my hair?"

Cassie looks at me like the idea is ridiculous. "I don't know how. I've only ever braided my own hair."

"You can do it." I nudge her leg—the leg with the scar. And then I take a risk and touch it. Cassie pulls away from me for a second and then eases her leg back to my hand. "Please," I say.

She groans and stands up. "Wait here."

Cassie comes back to the dock with a comb and a handful of rubber bands she collected in the cabin.

"How many braids are you going to put in my hair?"

"You'll see." Her face puckers into a snarky grin.

Cassie's fingers run over my scalp, separating hair into sections that she ties into little ponytails. She goes one by one, braiding each all the way to the end.

As she combs and thumbs and touches my hair, I get sleepy and calm. She doesn't say much as she works. Between the sun and the swimming and this, I could fall asleep.

In a half-dreamy state, I say, "I wish I could have done this with Molly. Sisters are supposed to braid each other's hair."

Cassie ties a rubber band around one of the braids. "I'm sorry about your sister, Z." And judging by Cassie's soft voice, she means it.

"I'm sorry about your life, Cassie."

"Me, too."

When my whole head is in braids, Cassie sits back down next to me on the end of the dock and stares off at Lake Kimball.

"What does the bottom of the lake feel like?"

"You've felt it."

"Not here," she says and then points out to the raft. "There."

I nod, finally understanding. "The sand is softer out there and there's less lake weed."

"That sounds nice."

"It is."

Cassie takes a moment and turns to me. "I want to touch the bottom. I want to jump off the raft. I want to be green," she says. "Will you help me?"

I run my hands over all the braids on my head. "Of course."

As Cassie and I are walking off the dock for the day, Hannah comes running up to us with letters in her hands.

"From home." She hands one to me and one to Cassie. In this moment, I realize I've never seen Cassie get a letter before.

"Thanks," I say.

Cassie holds the letter tight between her fingers. She doesn't look at me but stares off, her eyes wide.

"Cassie?"

She snaps out of it. "I'll meet you back at the cabin. I'm gonna hit the bathroom in the mess hall." When she's halfway up the stairs, she turns around. "By the way, Hannah, I know it was you."

Hannah gasps. "You told her!"

I shake my head and stutter over my words.

"No," Cassie yells, turning back around on the stairs. "You just did." She flings her towel over her shoulder. I keep my eyes on the letter grasped tightly in Cassie's hand. She's holding it like she's afraid it might blow away in the wind and disappear.

CHAPTER 25

Dear Zander,

Thank you for your letters. Your dad and I are so happy you are getting along well at camp. We are so happy. See. I'm trying.

The truth is, Zander, I thought I would be prepared. I thought I would be prepared for your sister to die. But I wasn't. I don't think parents are ever prepared, because no matter what the situation, we always hope it won't actually happen. It's foolish, I know. But the alternative . . . well, sometimes hope is the only alternative because the reality is too much.

It was too much.

I couldn't let go of Molly. When you have kids, and I pray you do some day, I hope you won't want to let them go either.

I knew it was wrong to keep her with me. But she was my baby. And I needed her until the very last day.

I still need her.

And I still need you.

Maybe there is something to this letter writing. I feel better just putting that down on paper.

I told Cooper you have a new boyfriend at camp and that you said this guy's a good kisser. I never liked Cooper anyway. He eats like a Neanderthal.

Love,

Mom

I hug my mom's letter to my chest, the paper crinkling around my hands. I lean against the outside of the mess hall as campers file in for dinner. I can't seem to put it away. I need to hold it for just a little while longer as her words settle in.

I reread the letter one more time.

"That better not be from Coop trying to get you back." Grover peers over my shoulder. I fold it quickly and stuff it in my back pocket. "Nice hair." He touches a braid.

"Cassie did it," I say, running my hand over my head. "The letter is from my mom."

"Did you tell her about me?"

"Maybe." I give Grover a half grin. We don't move. He picks up another one of my braids and spins it around his finger. Shivers cover my arms.

Grover's eyes sparkle more than usual tonight, and he's wearing his "Having fun isn't hard when you have a library card" shirt again. And the longer Grover looks at me, the more the butterflies flutter in my stomach.

"Will you do something with me tonight?" he asks.

I don't ask him what it is because I don't care. I just say yes, and we walk into the mess hall holding hands.

"And leave the braids. I like them."

Cassie is already sitting at our table. I didn't see her back at the cabin. I left early to read my mom's letter. There were too many eyes in one place. But seeing her now sends a surprising rush of relief through me.

When I pass the bin of apples, I run my hands over the fruit. I don't need one tonight. The memory of why plays on constant repeat in my head. That's good enough for right now. When I sit down next to Cassie, I offer her my roll.

"No, thanks, Z." Cassie pokes at her lettuce with her spoon.

"We can practice diving tomorrow," I say. "I can show you how to do it."

"Great. Can't wait."

Cassie doesn't say much through dinner, and her food stays mostly untouched. At one point she looks at Bek.

"Didn't your dead mother teach you not to smack your lips while you eat, Baby Fat?"

Bek looks at Cassie with big eyes. He swallows down his food in one big gulp. The comment isn't that off for Cassie, but her tone was different.

"Are you okay?" I ask.

She finally looks at me. "We've covered this, like, a million times, Z. I'm never okay." Then she smiles and the relief is back.

"So who was your letter from?" I take sip of my milk.

Cassie jabs a piece of lettuce with her spoon. "My Aunt Chey."

"I didn't know you had an aunt."

"Most people have aunts, Z." Cassie stabs at her plate again.

I can tell Cassie doesn't want to talk about it, so I drop it. At least she told me who the letter is from. That's something. And if there's one thing I've learned about Cassie, it's that I can't force her into anything.

After dinner and the nightly medication distribution, we have another bonfire of butchering James Taylor songs while Hayes plays guitar. Kerry asks if any of us want to come up and sing a solo.

"As a practice of *courage*," he says. "It takes guts to sing in front of a group."

To my surprise, Dori actually raises her hand. She sings an entire verse of "Fire and Rain." Her voice is light and sweet. Dori is probably in choir back in Chicago. I shift in my seat at the thought of going home. I'm comfortable with so much now, but that . . . I touch the letter in my pocket. This is as close as I want to be to Arizona right now.

As we head back to our cabins, Grover comes up behind me and pulls on my shirt.

"Remember you said you'd do me tonight," he whispers.

"I believe you're missing a word in that sentence."

"Two words, actually." Grover pulls on my shirt again. "You're not opposed to breaking and entering, are you?"

"Why?" I ask.

"You'll see." He starts to run back toward the boys' side of camp. "Just wait for me."

"Where?"

He stops. "In your bed, duh. Where else are we going to do it?"

All of the girls, including Cassie, fall asleep quickly, but I lie staring at the bunk above me, eyes wide open. I glance at the closed bathroom window. Madison reported to maintenance that it was missing the screw that keeps it closed, but they said they'd fix it at the end of the summer. In the meantime, she put tape along the bottom.

I can see Madison's face as she sleeps. Her long hair falls in front of her shoulder by the key dangling from her neck, and for a brief moment, I wonder what her broken pieces are. No one is perfect. Even when you have the key needed to get out of a locked room, that doesn't mean you use it. Some people are more comfortable stuck in their own traps.

The minutes feel heavy as I wait for Grover, like every tick takes longer to get to the tock. When I hear the door click, I sit up. The door opens so slightly that anyone who wasn't looking for it wouldn't notice, but I do. Because I've been waiting. And, turns out, waiting isn't so bad.

I put on my tennis shoes and tiptoe over to the door. As quietly as possible, I slip through and into the night.

Grover stands in the moonlight, wearing plaid pajama pants and a white T-shirt.

"How did you open the door?" I ask.

He holds up a gigantic ring with a zillion keys on it. "I brought my keys."

"How did you get those?"

"I stole the master set last year and made copies after I got home. It has to be a fire hazard to lock us in every night. I know the camp ensures safety for all the campers, but I'm just not comfortable with that."

That explains how he was able to sneak out. "Did you give Cassie the key to the Wellness Center?"

Grover nods. "She was in need."

"I thought Madison had the only key." I touch the ring.

"There's never only *one* key that unlocks a door, Zander." Grover puts his arm around me. "Come on. I want to show you something."

As we walk over to the mess hall, Grover doesn't let go of me. He pulls me into his side in the nook of his arm. He uses one of his keys, unlocks the door, and pulls me through the dark mess hall, keeping me close to him.

We stop at a closet door.

"We snuck out to hide in a broom closet?" I whisper and yawn.

The room is dark but I can see Grover smile. He pushes the door back. Light comes from an illuminated TV screen. On the floor are pillows set up like chairs, and a bowl of popcorn sits in between them.

"What is this?"

Grover pulls me into the room. "A date to see a movie."

"A date." I smile at Grover.

"I saw Kerry store the TV in here and I got to thinking . . . Unfortunately, the theater has a limited selection of movies. And there's the added risk of getting arrested."

I sit down on one of the pillows. "I'll take the risk."

Grover presses play on the DVD player and sits down next to me. I pick up the popcorn, resting my head on his shoulder.

"I know it just started, but I can already tell that this is going to be the best date I've ever been on," I say.

"This is the only date I've ever been on," Grover says.

"Seriously?"

Grover's gaze moves to his hands. He pulls on the bottom of his shirt. "A schizophrenic dad prone to losing his pants isn't really a chick magnet. The truth is that most people are afraid of my dad, Zander."

I grab Grover's hand and squeeze. "People were afraid of Molly, too. Sometimes reality is just too ugly to look at."

Grover's eyes finally come back to me. "There is no way what I am looking at right now could ever be considered ugly."

His words make me want to burst into tears and laughter.

"So what's playing at the movie theater tonight?" I ask.

"A true teen classic. *The Breakfast Club*."

I toss a piece of popcorn into my mouth. "I've heard good things about this one."

The movie's music starts and we both settle back onto the pillows, but Grover doesn't let go of my hand. He holds it tight and places it right on top of his heart.

When the movie ends, neither Grover nor I move. My head rests on his chest, my arm drapes across his torso, and my leg hooks over his lower half. I'm tangled up in Grover.

He plays with my braids as the credits roll over a frozen picture of John Bender shoving his fist high in the air on the football field.

"Do you think the prom queen and the criminal stay together when they go back to school on Monday?" I ask.

"I hope so," Grover says.

"I hope so, too." I fiddle with his shirt, twisting it between my fingers. "Are you really a virgin, Grover?" He sits up, which makes me do the same. I sit back on my knees, facing him, and shrug. "It was just such a big deal in the movie."

"Yes." Grover's voice is even. "I'm a virgin."

His words cause me to exhale.

"Did you and Cooper . . ." Grover trails off.

"No. He just liked my boobs."

"I can see why."

I know I'm blushing now, but I don't let my eyes drift from Grover's face. I steady my breath and gather the courage I need to confess something. Courage like Madison talked about. "I never really *felt* Cooper when we messed around. Not really. I just did it because it made my parents think everything was okay. If I was making out and going to school and getting good grades then I wasn't drowning."

"Selfishly, I'm glad you never really felt Cooper."

I scoot my knees closer to him on the broom closet floor.

"So this is kind of like the first time I've ever done something like this with a boy."

"This is kind of the first time I've done something like this with a girl," Grover says.

When I hear his words, I know what I need to do next. I take a deep breath. *Courage.* I reach for the back pocket of his pants. *Courage.* I search for his notebook but I can't find it.

"Where's your notebook?" I ask.

Grover's eyes don't leave mine when he says, "I'm trying to survive without it."

Courage.

No matter what the odds are of Grover and I being together past this moment in time, right now I am 100 percent positive this is where I'm meant to be. This is worth living for.

I grab the bottom of my shirt and close my eyes. I don't want to be numb anymore. Anywhere. I want the courage to feel. Everything. I *need* it.

I pull my shirt over my head and set it on the ground next to us. I do the same with my bra. And then I'm bare. My chest flutters with every breath. The skin that covers my heart and my lungs and all the things that make me alive inside is exposed. I peel my eyes open slowly.

Grover takes me in for only a moment before he takes off his own shirt. I've seen his chest before—I even saw it today while we were swimming—but here, in this place, it's different.

I take my hand, my fingers unsteady, and place it on his heart. He shakes as he touches me, doing the same. Grover presses his palm into my skin.

"Can you feel me?" he asks.

I nod. I feel every inch of his hand, down to the ridges and curves of his fingerprints, like they're etched in me.

I pull his hand from my chest and set it on my shoulder. I start at the top of his arm and move slowly as I make my way down, drawing circles with my fumbling fingers over his skin. He feels so smooth and I'm not. I'm broken and shaking and scared, but I won't back away. Because Grover is all of those things, too.

He closes his eyes and bites his bottom lip. When I get to his fingers, I bring his hand up to my mouth and kiss it. I kiss every fingertip and make a wish. I wish he never gets sick. I wish he remembers this for the rest of his life. I wish him a real life for the *rest* of his life, the ugly and all. Because reality might be ugly, but sometimes we can be broken *and* beautiful.

When I pull Grover toward me, he opens his eyes. His hand comes to the side of my face and travels to my braided hair. He tucks one braid behind my ear and it pops back out.

"You can't be contained," he says.

"Not tonight."

"No, Zander. Not ever."

I kiss him then, my lips pressing against his. My body rises to meet Grover's, and we melt into one. His fingers press into my back as mine trail the length of his spine. My lips search his for every taste that might be there. For every inch of every word and sound that has ever crossed Grover's lips.

We lie back on the pillows, warm skin against warm skin. I giggle when Grover nips at my neck.

This night will never end because for every moment of every day for the rest of my life, I will relive it. It will always sit on the surface, floating.

CHAPTER 26

To Whom It May Concern,
I reject your ruling.
Kisses,
Cassandra Dakota LaSalle

My shirt is still lying on the floor. My fingers search the area for my bra. I lift up Grover's arm, slide underneath it, and set it back down across his bare stomach.

He sleeps with his mouth slightly open, breathing half through his nose, half through his mouth. I bite my bottom lip as a fire ignites in my stomach. I feel like I could burst into a million wonderful, jagged, broken pieces.

As my clothes go over my skin, the fabric touching all the places Grover did hours earlier, I hum. My body zings with life.

I peer out the crack in the broom closet door. The trees are shadowed in light gray and purple with the faintest hint of yellow. There isn't much time.

"Grover." I touch his cheek. He moves his face into my hand. "Grover," I say, trying to coax him out of sleep.

He takes my hand and slowly, like a blind person, starts feeling his way up my arm, but his eyes don't open.

"Please tell me you're real. That this wasn't a dream. That I'm not going to open my eyes and be back in my bed in my room with a lame Spider-Man poster hanging on my wall."

"You have a Spider-Man poster on your wall?"

"Comics are cool." Grover's hands come up to my face.

"I'm real."

He opens his eyes. "And I'm finally found."

Grover walks me back to my cabin as the sun starts to show in the sky. At the door, he stops. "So I guess I'll call you." He rubs his hand through his hair.

"Grover, you'll see me in, like, two hours."

"Just play along. It's our first date, remember?"

I smile. "I had a really nice time."

"Me, too. Maybe we could do it again sometime?" Grover offers me his hand to shake. I take it.

"I'd like that."

He yanks me toward him and kisses me. "By the way," he whispers in my ear. "I still think the prom queen and the criminal stay together."

I smile, feeling his breath on my ear. Then I reach behind myself and unclip my bra. Grover looks at me like he's totally confused and yet completely intrigued. I pull my arms inside my shirt and slide the bra off my shoulders. Then, like a magician pulling a colorful line of handkerchiefs from a hat, I produce it through one of the armholes of my shirt.

"I don't have a diamond earring. This will have to do."

I kiss him good night or maybe it's good morning and slip back into my cabin.

"You look weird," Cassie says from behind me.

I yawn into my hand as we go down the food line. I barely hear her.

"Good morning, ladies," Grover comes up behind us. His hair is wet and he smells like soap. "Or should I say lady and . . . What are you today, Sticks, boy or girl?"

"Tired."

"Well, at least you're something." Grover tilts his head at me. "And how about you, Zander, how are you?"

Before I can get a word out, Cassie goes around me in line, bumping her tray into my back.

"She's acting weird."

"Weird, you say?" Grover puts his finger on the bottom of his chin. I remember kissing it, feeling a little patch of stubble with my tongue. Shivers cover my arms.

"Great," I finally say. "I'm great."

"Great." He smiles.

"Great." I nod.

"Great." Cassie says exaggeratedly. "I'm gonna go vomit."

Grover clicks his tongue at her. "Sticks, that isn't your style."

Cassie walks away without a word.

Grover and I just stare at each other. His skin has a clean sheen to it, almost like he's wax. Last night doesn't feel real. I reach up and touch his wet hair, just to make sure. He does the same to one of my braids.

Kerry claps three times, the sound reverberating through the mess hall, and I jump.

"The only way to be found," Kerry yells.

I take my hand away from Grover's hair. "Is to admit we're lost," I say.

"Amen." Grover winks. He grabs an apple out of the fruit bin and tosses it into the air. I catch it.

"An apple a day," he says.

"Keeps the doctor away."

"God, I hope that's true."

All during breakfast, Grover's hand rests on my thigh. None of us say much. My head feels heavy on my neck, and the spot where Grover is touching me is warm. He bites into the apple, and it cracks open like a log being split. He offers me a bite, but I shake my head. Grover needs it more than I do.

When Kerry dismisses everyone, Grover says, "Archery. I think I'm interested in archery this morning. I believe overnight my aim has improved. I might actually hit the target today."

"Me, too," I say as Cassie gets up from the table without a word. "And we'll swim this afternoon?"

"Whatever, Katniss." She starts to walk away.

I smile at Grover.

But as we walk to archery, I stop for a moment. I didn't notice what Cassie had for breakfast, but she must have eaten something. And the diet pills are still in her bag.

Grover grabs my hand and gives it a tug toward him. He pins me against a tree and snaps a green leaf free from a branch. He traces the length of my arm with it, brushing it against my skin like a feather.

"Can you feel that?"

Before I can even nod, his lips connect with mine, and any questions I have about Cassie or anything else drift far away.

"I can't do it!" Cassie yells as her head pops out of the water.

"Yes, you can." I yawn into my hand. A fatigue-induced tear rolls down my cheek and I wipe it way. I pull a memory from last night to the surface to help trudge through the rest of the day, like a caffeine shot. But the longer this swim lesson goes on, the less the memories work.

"No. I. Can't." Cassie annunciates every word.

I sit back on my hands on the dock. The sun beats down on my face. I point to the yellow diving stick sitting on the bottom of Lake Kimball.

"It's right there. Try again."

Cassie pushes out an exasperated breath before diving back under. I close my eyes for a second and use the memory of Grover tracing my collarbone with his fingertips from one of my shoulders to another to keep me going. My stomach pulls in tight at the thought. I touch my lips and remember the salt from the popcorn and the way his arms covered in shivers when I kissed the soft spot right behind his ear.

"You're not even watching me!" My eyes fly open. Cassie stands in water up to her shoulders in the yellow zone. "What if I was drowning?"

"Stop being dramatic. Madison is right there." I point to the beach where she stands with a red life preserver hugged to her chest.

"Mads is not going to save me."

"Well, maybe you should have been nicer to her. She's not that bad."

"Maybe you should have been watching me."

I ignore the jab. "Did you get the diving stick?"

"No. I can't find it," Cassie says.

"Just open your eyes under the water."

"I'm not opening my eyes in this cesspool." Cassie points at a glistening Lake Kimball. "I'll get pinkeye."

"No you won't. That's not how you get pinkeye anyway." I yawn again.

"Why are you so tired?" Cassie asks.

"I didn't sleep well." It's not a lie, but the uncomfortable feeling in my gut tells me it's not exactly the truth either. I wipe away the sweat beading on my forehead and change the subject. "Just hold your breath, slowly blowing bubbles out of your nose on your way down to the bottom. When you see the ring, grab it, and then push your feet as hard as you can off of the lake floor to make your way back to the surface."

"You make it sound easy."

"It *is* easy." My shoulders slump and my voice carries a sharper tone.

"What if I can't make it?"

"Just come back up."

"You make *that* sound so easy," Cassie snaps. Her voice is tight in her throat. "But it's not that easy to just keep coming up to the surface for air. It's tiring. And the farther I get to the bottom the harder it is to get back up. And then what if I can't. What if I just can't get to the surface anymore?"

"You can do it." I sound unconvincing.

"What if I can't?"

"Then I'll jump in and save you."

"You were just closing your eyes," Cassie barks. "You can't always be there to save me, Zander, and you won't."

"Then don't do it!" I yell, standing up on the dock, exhausted. The sun is just so hot on my skin and my eyes are blurry from sweat and I can't seem to find a memory that makes this better. "I don't care!"

Cassie takes a step back from me in the water. "You don't care?"

I run my hands through my braided hair. "Look, let's skip the lesson for today. We'll work on it tomorrow."

"You're quitting on me?"

"You make it sound like I'm abandoning you," I say.

"Are you?" Cassie's eyes are fierce.

"I'm just trying so hard and you make it so difficult."

"I'm sorry to be *difficult.*"

I pick up my towel, trying to ignore her goading.

"So you're just giving up on me?" Cassie snaps.

"God, Cassie. Why does it always have to be about you? It's not all about you," I yell again. "You're so fucking selfish."

Cassie's jaw gets tight and she takes another step back. "Maybe I'm selfish because no one ever gives a shit. I'm the only one who cares about me."

I blow out an exaggerated breath and roll my eyes. I'm too tired for this conversation. "Let's just try this again tomorrow."

Cassie climbs out of the water. "Fine. That's fine." She runs her shoulder into me as she walks down the dock, mumbling something about today being all we have, but the words get lost in my head as soon as they enter, disappearing into a cloud of fatigue.

CHAPTER 27

Cher Papa,
J'ai embrassé une fille et je l'aime.
Cordialement,
Alex Trebek

When I get back to the cabin, Dori is sleeping in her bunk. I fall into my bed. Dori sleeps a lot, but I don't think we're tired for the same reason. She said in group share-apy that she's literally tired of life. She sleeps so she doesn't have to deal with it. Today, I'm tired for the opposite reason.

The pillow cradles my head. I pull my lousy sheet up to my ears, ignoring the bitter remnants of my fight with Cassie that circle around in my mind and focusing on the better ones—Grover skimming his fingers over every vertebra in my back. Me kissing my way from the top of his forehead to his lips and to his chin and down his neck. The bed gets warm as my limbs melt into the hard mattress. I coax more memories out—my tongue tracing the inside of his mouth. Grover kissing my stomach. And then I'm gone.

I wake up when it's time for dinner, peeling my face off of my pillow. My head hurts from being in one position, and my braids are mashed down on the side of my head.

I pull out the braids and splash water on my face before heading to the mess hall.

Cassie stands outside, pacing the deck, like an armed soldier keeping guard. When I get closer, I see that she's reading something.

"Is that the letter from your aunt?" I ask.

Cassie whips around and crumbles the paper into a ball in her hand.

"Like you care." I can't stop my eyes from rolling. Cassie looks at my hair. "And you took out your braids."

"They were hurting my head." My voice is flat.

"Whatever." She shoves the letter into her pocket and pushes past me into the mess hall.

The tension between us doesn't ease when we sit down. Grover looks at Cassie and me across the table. "So how did the lesson go?"

"It didn't," Cassie says. "Thanks to little Miss I-Need-A-Fucking-Nap."

"I was tired." I glance at Grover out of the corner of my eye.

"From being up all night?" Bek chimes in, his mouth full of food. He reaches over the table and takes my chocolate milk. I stare down at my tray, unable to look at Cassie.

"What?" Cassie sounds genuinely surprised.

"Grover and Zander were up all night." Bek takes a sip of my milk.

"Give that back to me." I snatch the cup from his hands. Little bits of food float at the top. "Gross." I hand it back to him.

"Is he lying?" Cassie's words come through her teeth.

"You told him?" I ask Grover.

"He woke up when I came back in the cabin. I couldn't lie to him. Then it would be like I condone lying, which I don't, and then he might start lying again." Grover shrugs.

"You snuck out without me?" Cassie scoots her chair away from me. I glare at Bek and don't say anything. "So you couldn't teach me today because you were up all night giving Cleve a bad blow job? You said you'd help me."

"What do you think I've been doing all summer?" I blurt out and stab the macaroni and cheese on my plate.

"So I've been your charity case?" Cassie asks.

"That's not what I said. Stop twisting my words."

"I don't know who the real liar is now. Bek or Zander."

"I didn't lie to you," I say.

"No, you just didn't include me, which is worse than lying."

Cassie gets up and slams her chair under the table. We all sit in silence as she stalks out of the mess hall. I look from Grover to Bek, tired and sick of always chasing after Cassie when she has a fit. Grover looks guilty. But no one goes after her.

It isn't until we're cleaning up that I realize she didn't have any food on her tray.

CHAPTER 28

Dear Aunt Chey,

Courage: To summon bravery within oneself. To do something you never thought you could do. To face the truth. To act with confidence. To finally admit what your life is and will always be. To see the end and know it.

Cassie

When I get back to the cabin that night, I find the University of Arizona sweatshirt and Molly's quilt on my bed. I pack them away in my bag and stuff it under the bunk bed.

Cassie stays silent. She doesn't say a word to any of us, not even Grover. A day passes and another. My stubborn side comes out—the side that kept me quiet for so many years with Molly. The side that made me numb. Cassie and I sit across from each other at meals, but I grind my teeth and choke on my words. I spend my time at archery and arts and crafts. We don't swim.

And Grover watches it all. He slides his hand over my thigh under the table, helping to ease everything inside of me, but I still stay silent.

In the cabin, I write letters to my parents and talk to Dori about her plans to confront her mom when she gets home.

"I'm gonna ask to live with my dad," she says. "I don't care if he lives on the other side of the country and I'll have to make new friends. My friends kind of suck anyway."

I glance at Cassie, who's peeling nail polish from her toenails.

"That sounds like a good plan."

"I'm just tired of being tired," Dori says. "What about you? What are you going to do when you get home?"

"Home?" I don't even like saying the word. "I haven't really thought about it."

In the morning, I find Grover leaning against a picnic bench outside of my cabin.

"Grover, you're not supposed to be over here," Madison says.

"What would humanity be if all anyone ever did was what they were supposed to do? Jesus was *supposed* to be a carpenter. What would have happened if he didn't break the rules and become the Son of God?"

Madison shakes her head and laughs. "It's too early for this."

The rest of the cabin walks toward the mess hall, but Cassie lingers in the back of the group and glares at us as she passes. I do the same back to her.

I lean back on the picnic table next to Grover. He takes my hand. "And the power play goes on."

I ignore the comment.

He lifts my hand and places it directly on top of his. His fingers extend more than a knuckle past mine. I press my palm into his until both our hands are touching entirely, and the anger I feel toward Cassie melts away. I sigh and lay my head on Grover's arm.

"Fancy a game of tetherball before breakfast?" he asks.

"Against you?" Grover nods and I smile. "You're on."

We walk over to the tetherball court by the mess hall. The ball hangs from the pole, dangling in the breeze.

"You can start," Grover says.

I take the ball from him, thoroughly prepared to kick his ass. We've never played, but I beat Bek just last week, even though he told me he was the Tetherball Champion of Canada.

"Ready?" I ask.

"Ready."

I pull my arm back and lift the ball high in the air. I smack it with as much force as I can. Grover jumps when it gets to his side of the court and stops the ball with one of his hands. He tosses it back at me. It soars over my head and out of arm's reach. When it gets back to his side, he does it again and again and again, until the ball wraps tightly around the pole and he wins.

I put my hands on my hips. "Best two out of three."

Grover smiles as he unwraps the ball from the pole. "You can start again."

I take the same stance and the game begins. When the ball smacks against the pole, announcing Grover's win for a second time, I stomp my foot.

"But that's unfair. You're taller than me and you have big hands."

"Why, thank you." He gives me one of his winks. "Why do you care so much about winning anyway?"

"I don't."

"You don't?"

"No . . ." I take a step back from the court, my adrenaline from the game fizzling out. "Maybe . . ."

"Maybe what?"

"You're tricking me."

"Me?"

I sit down on the ground. Grover takes the seat next to me. He picks up my hand again and traces the outline of it with his finger. I don't ever want this summer to end.

"Someone has to be the bigger person." He presses his palm to mine. "See."

I lean my head on his shoulder. "Yes. I see." He doesn't let go of my hand. "You know you could have just said that."

"That's boring. Plus, I like seeing you jump."

I nudge him in the side.

In the mess hall, I stop with my tray of food behind our table. Cassie's back is to me. Grover taps my back with his tray to move me forward. I try not to groan as I take a seat next to her.

I eat half of my meal, every few bites glancing at Cassie. She takes a few sips of water as she peels an orange one bit at a time. When the skin is off, she pulls each slice apart, but not a single one goes in her mouth.

"Aren't you going to eat it?" I ask.

She doesn't say anything, but takes one of the slices and slams her hand down on it, crushing it flat. A piece of pulp lands on my cheek and I wipe it away.

"You need to eat, Cassie."

"You're not my mother." She smashes another one.

"I can see you're making fresh-squeezed orange juice this morning, Sticks. How healthy of you," Grover adds. "I hear vitamin C is all the rage."

She doesn't say anything.

"Maslow says you need to eat," I qualify.

"I don't give a shit about Maslow."

"Then do it for me."

Cassie looks at me with blazing eyes. "Why would I do anything for you?"

I take a breath. Durga, Durga, Durga. I remind myself to be a warrior. "Because I care about you," I say.

Cassie cackles in her seat, tossing her head back. She laughs like I've just cracked the biggest joke she's ever heard.

"You don't care about me."

"Yes, I do." I touch her arm.

"No touching, remember." Cassie smiles at me with clenched teeth. It's not a real smile, but more like she's challenging me and she's getting a kick out of it. She raises her hand, yelling for Kerry.

"Yes, Cassie," he says.

"I'd like to acknowledge something this morning." Cassie speaks loud enough that the whole mess hall goes silent and turns toward our table.

"You'd like to acknowledge something." He repeats it like he's clarifying something he misheard.

Cassie nods and stands up from her seat, glaring down at me.

"I know why Zander was sent to camp."

The moment the words come out of her mouth, my stomach dives to the floor and I freeze in my seat. I can't even bring my arm up to yank her down. And then it all comes out in one waterfall of words.

"Cassie, that's not—" Kerry tries to say, but her booming voice cuts him off.

"She almost drowned at a swim meet because she was so sad about her dead sister who died choking on an apple. And her fat-ass coach had to give her mouth to mouth. I was right. She was an apathetic mess who was dead on the inside . . . just like her sister." Cassie's vacant eyes haven't left me. I feel a tear roll down my cheek and plop on my bare knee. And Cassie just watches it fall.

I run out of the mess hall, pushing the doors as hard as I can, and take off toward the archery field. I need to disappear into the woods and hide in the trees. I choke on my breath as I trip over a root poking out of the ground, but Grover grabs my arm, catching me before I fall. I didn't know he was behind me.

"How could she?" I say with ragged breath. "How could she?"

Grover picks me up and presses me to him. He kisses my cheeks and forehead and nose.

"I'm sorry," he says into my ear. "I'm sorry."

He brushes my hair out of my face, keeping his hands on my cheeks. A fire lights in my stomach as what Cassie just did settles in. It burns and hurts.

"I did what you asked. All I've worried about is what Cassie needs." I pace back and forth in front of Grover. My voice grows louder with the more words I say. "But what about me? I'm happy for the first time in years, maybe ever. I'm happy! And she's ruining it. She is ruining my happiness." I stop in my tracks, reality coming clear in my mind. "She's broken, Grover. I can't save her. You can't save her. No one can save her. She's broken and she'll stay that way forever."

After the words fall out of my mouth, the sound of someone approaching us catches my attention.

I turn to find Cassie standing in the trees, her jaw jutting forward as she bites down hard.

"I was coming to apologize," she says.

I freeze.

"You think I'm broken . . . forever." Cassie says my own words back at me. I step toward her, but she moves away. "You know what? I don't need you." And then she starts running.

Grover and I finally catch up to Cassie down on the beach. She's fast when she wants to be. She walks straight up to Madison and says, "I want to test for green."

"What?" Madison says.

"Are you deaf, Mads? I want to test for green."

I grab on to Cassie's arm. "What are you doing?"

She yanks out of my grip. "I don't need you."

"Sticks."

Cassie points at Grover. "Or you."

"Are you sure you want to do this?" Madison asks.

"Just test me." Cassie pushes past us and goes out onto the dock. Madison hesitates for a moment and then grabs the diving sticks from inside the equipment shed and walks out to meet her. I stand on the beach next to Grover, biting my nails.

Cassie strips down to her bathing suit. When I can't take it anymore, I grab Grover's hand and pull him out onto the dock.

"Don't do this, Cassie," I yell at her.

"Put the stick in the lake," Cassie barks at Madison.

And Madison does it. I look at her like she's crazy. Cassie will drown and Madison knows it. Cassie's barely been able to get one stick out of six feet let alone twelve feet.

"It's okay, Zander, I won't let anything happen," Madison says. She turns to Cassie. "You have to get the stick and bring it back to the surface."

I watch as Cassie nods and squeezes her hands at her side.

"Please, Cassie." I try one last time.

She looks me dead in the eyes. "You don't believe in me."

And then Cassie jumps in.

I pull in a breath as her body hits the water. Grover grabs my hand as Cassie's pink bathing suit disappears from the surface and goes lower into the blue. I count the seconds in my head. One . . . two . . . three . . . I hold air tight in my lungs. Four . . . five . . . six . . . I peer over the side of the dock. My nerves spike.

"Come on," I whisper. "Come on."

But Cassie doesn't come back up, and the seconds tick on longer.

"This isn't good," Grover says.

Madison takes off the shirt that's covering her bathing suit. "I'm going in to get her." And a second later, she dives in after Cassie.

I grab on to Grover and pray. I pray to St. Anthony of Padua that the lost be found. That the soul be free. That life be everlasting. And that Cassie makes it back up to the surface.

I say it over three times before Madison pops back up with Cassie in her arms. They both gasp for breath. Madison drags Cassie over to the dock as Grover reaches down for her. Cassie slumps over and coughs water out of her nose and mouth.

"Are you okay?" I ask, wiping water from Cassie's face and hair.

"I didn't make it," she says and coughs. "I didn't make it."

"It's okay, Cassie." I begin to wipe more water from her skin, but Cassie backs away from my touch. She stands up on the dock, her knees shaky and her chest heaving in ragged breaths.

"No it's not." She pushes past me, knocking my arm with so much force I fall down.

Madison sits winded on the end of the dock, a shocked look on her face. "She almost drowned," she says. "I can't believe she almost drowned."

I watch Cassie run up the stairs, wobbly on her legs and dripping with water. She disappears into the trees around the mess hall.

I don't see Cassie again until dinner. I wait for her in the cabin, rolling Hannah's gimp key chain around in my hand. The melted end is starting to fray and come apart. Madison said courage takes multiple forms. That it doesn't have to be skydiving or bungee jumping. That for some people just getting up every day is an act of courage. That the smallest act can have the biggest effect.

I get the University of Arizona sweatshirt out of my bag. It feels like I've stolen it from Cassie, and she needs to have it. One small gesture of courage—I put it on her bed.

Cassie isn't in the mess hall when I arrive for dinner. I go through the line and sit down, my eyes watching the door for her. When she finally appears, I touch Grover's leg.

She grabs a tray and walks down the line of food. Her body looks different. Cassie normally walks with her chest out, but tonight her shoulders round down toward the ground. Even her neck seems to hang lower. She passes all of the food, never putting an item on her tray.

I press my hand into Grover's thigh and wait for Cassie to sit down with us. At the end of the line, she turns to face the entire mess hall of campers. Many are staring at her, the news of what happened traveling fast.

Cassie blinks and looks around the room before walking over to Madison. The room is so quiet everyone can hear what she says.

"I don't feel well, Madison. Can I go lie down for the night?" A look of complete shock washes over Madison's face as she fumbles with her words. "Can I, please?"

Madison nods quickly. Cassie sets her empty tray down on the table and walks out of the mess hall.

"I miss her already," Bek says, staring at Cassie's empty seat.

"What do we do?" I look at Grover.

"I'm not sure it's about us anymore." Grover exhales. "It was never about us."

When I get back to the cabin, Cassie is there. She lies with her back to me, the University of Arizona sweatshirt back on my bed.

No one says anything as we brush our teeth. Cassie doesn't move, except for her back going up and down with inhales and exhales. I glance at her every few seconds.

When the cabin goes dark and I'm in my bed, I say, "Good night, Cassie."

She doesn't respond. I hug her sweatshirt to my chest and press it to my nose. It smells like her.

A nightmare shakes me awake. Or a memory. I sit up straight in the middle of the night.

"She called her Madison," I whisper. "She called her Madison." My stomach churns. I look at Cassie's bed. She's gone. The bathroom window is open and letting the smallest breeze through the slight crack. I get Cassie's duffel bag from under her bed and rip open the side pocket with her diet pills. They're gone. All of them. My heart pounds loud in my ears.

"I need the key!" I scream as I shake Madison awake. "I need the key!"

Madison looks at me, confused and scared. She yanks the key from around her neck, breaking the chain, and hands it over.

I run to the door as everyone stirs in the cabin, my hands shaking as I try to force the key into the lock.

"Get me out of here!" I scream. Madison is at my side in a second. She takes the key and slides it in with ease. The door pops open. I don't wait for permission. I take off toward the lake, my feet barely able to keep up with my torso.

"I pray that the lost be found. That the soul be free. That life be everlasting."

At the mess hall, I stumble down the stairs toward the beach. My toe stubs on something, but I barely feel it. All I feel are my fingers squeezing the sweatshirt in my hands as tight as I can as I run.

My feet hit the sand, slowing me down, but I fight forward.

Madison said that sometimes people misuse courage.

I run to where the water meets the land.

Sometimes people do things that are harmful and hurtful because they're scared or lonely or desperate.

I look out at Lake Kimball, my hands numb and my heart on the verge of exploding. Tears streak my face.

They call it *courage.*

I see bottles floating on the surface of the water. Pill bottles.

I drop the sweatshirt on the ground. Cassie floats next to them. Facedown.

PERSEVERANCE

CHAPTER 29

Dear Mom and Dad,

When Molly was first in the hospital, you took me to see her. I walked into the room with all those machines. It was louder than I thought it would be. I asked you what I was supposed to do. You said to just talk to her like I always did. That she could hear me.

But I never talked to Molly other than when I helped Mom feed her. I'd tell her to open wide and then pretend the spoon was an airplane coming in for a landing.

She was small in the bed. I touched her legs and thought about how they would never walk again. And then I thought about all the words that we would never say to each other because as much as you didn't want to admit it, Molly wasn't waking up. She wasn't.

When my time was up in the room, you sent me outside to sit by myself. I sat leaning against the cold hospital wall, and all I could see in my head were Molly's little legs. And all I could think about was how much it hurt to know she'd never walk again. It hurt so badly, I wanted to rip my own legs off and give them to her.

Instead, I balled myself up. I pulled my legs into my chest and squeezed my arms around my knees and ground my teeth together. I closed my eyes so tightly I thought my eyelids might break. And I promised myself I would never *feel this bad again. I would* never *feel this bad again. I would* never *feel this bad again.*

Love,

Z

I dive into the water and swim as fast as I've ever swum. Faster than any meet. I flip Cassie's body over in the water. Her face is dark in the blackness around us and her eyes are closed. All that is illuminated in the night is her hot-pink bathing suit as I pull her back to shore.

I drag her up on the beach and start screaming for Grover. I scream over and over and over again. Then I start mouth to mouth. I don't know what I'm doing. I push air into Cassie and pump on her chest and nothing happens.

I scream for Grover again.

Someone grabs my arm. I flip my wet hair out of my face and find Madison. She pulls me off of Cassie, even though I fight against her. I scream mean words that I never thought I could scream, but Madison pushes me back on the sand.

"You don't give a shit about her! You want her dead! You want her dead!"

Madison ignores me and pushes Cassie's hair back on her face to start CPR. Real CPR.

I cry, sitting on the ground, my tears and the water on my clothes collecting sand. I yell for Grover again.

And then he's here. He's grabbing me and asking me what happened.

"You were supposed to watch her," I say to him. "You said you were going to watch her."

"I know, Zander. I'm so sorry." Grover grabs my face, but I need to see Cassie. I need to see *her*.

I push him back and try to get around Madison, but Kerry is here now, blocking my way. And Hayes. And everyone from my cabin.

Lights flash up the hill by the mess hall—red and white in the darkness. Men in uniforms run down to the beach, but they're all just blocking my view. I need to see her.

Grover tries to hold me back as I push at people and scream. This is what everyone wanted. They wanted me to feel and scream and cry, and now that I'm doing it, no one is listening to me.

"I *need* to see her," I say through ragged breaths to Grover. I grab on to his shirt and twist it between my fists. "I *need* to see her."

"I know, Zander." He takes me in his long arms and I melt into my tears, collapsing onto the sand in my sobs.

Cassie gets put on a long board, and the EMTs carry her quickly up the stairs. I scramble across the sand and get the sweatshirt.

"She needs her sweatshirt!" I yell after them. "She'll be cold when she wakes up."

Kerry steps in front of me as I'm about to race up the stairs and stops me. "Just let them do their job, Zander."

"But she needs this." I hold up her shirt. He doesn't understand that it's hers. He stands still, not budging from his place. I take a breath, trying to calm myself. "Please, let me go with her."

"I'm sorry but my answer is no."

"Please, Kerry." I grab on to him like a life jacket, like he's the only thing that has the power to keep me floating.

"I'll take her with me." Madison comes up next to us. "It's the right thing to do, Kerry."

He shakes his head and exhales, and at that moment I think it's over. I might never see Cassie again. Then Kerry nods. "Fine, but you're in charge of her. I'll meet you at the hospital."

I run up the stairs behind Madison, only stopping once to glance back at Grover, who sits on the beach with his head in his hands. When he smacks the ground, I feel a piece of my heart break into a million shards of glass.

Madison and I pass through the gates that divide Camp Padua from the rest of the world as the sun begins to rise.

CHAPTER 30

Dear Mom and President Cleveland,
I have failed. I must be impeached.
Your son,
Grover Cleveland

Every hospital smells the same, like cotton balls dipped in alcohol sprinkled with death.

The doctors won't let me back to see her. They say she's not awake anyway.

I sit next to Madison in one of the uncomfortable waiting room chairs, just breathing.

My clothes have dried and my hair hangs limp on my head. Limp. Like Cassie's body was.

"Is she going to die?"

Madison twists her fingers together. "I don't know."

"I don't want her to die."

"Contrary to what you think, neither do I."

"I'm sorry," I say. "I was scared. I didn't mean it."

Madison places her hand on my back. "It's okay."

"Why have you put up with Cassie this whole time?" I ask.

Madison exhales a long breath and says, "We all have our crazy, Zander."

"You don't seem to," I say.

Madison shakes her head. "I spent last spring break at the psych ward with my mom. It's the fourth time I've been called out of school to deal with her. My dad gave up years ago, but I just can't seem to."

I try not to act shocked but I am. Madison just seems so perfect.

"I know what my thing is now," I say. A smile grows on Madison's face. "It's Cassie."

"Make sure you tell her that." She stands up and motions down the hallway toward the cafeteria. "Do you want some coffee?"

"Coffee?"

"I figure since we're not on camp property anymore, we can have a little pick-me-up."

"Dori called coffee 'life support.'"

Madison nods. "Today, that just might be true."

"I'll take two cups."

"You got it." Madison musters a smile, but it doesn't reach her eyes, which look bloodshot and tired. She pats my shoulder. "When she wakes up, make sure to tell her what you told me."

"Which part?"

"The part where you said you don't want her to die." I start crying again, but nod at Madison through the tears. "Tell her I said the same thing," she says over her shoulder as she walks down the hallway to get us some life support.

Hours pass. Kerry shows up at the hospital. He doesn't look good. In fact, he looks terrible. His hair is matted to his head and his cheeks are splotched in red. Doctors come out and talk to him, and he nods and runs his hands through his hair and slumps his shoulders even more. I can't tell what anyone is saying, and it drives me even crazier than I already feel.

The doctors pull him behind the big automatic doors they took Cassie through before I can even get out of my chair. Madison pats my leg again. Five cups of coffee sit on the table in front of us.

Kerry is gone for a long time—too long. My knee bounces uncontrollably as my foot taps on the ground. When Kerry finally comes back, he walks over and looks at the cups.

"We needed it," Madison says before he can comment. Kerry nods.

"She's stable." When he says the words, my body collapses into itself. I go limp in the chair from holding on so strong. Blood rushes to my toes and I think I might pass out, but Madison grabs my hand and holds on tight. "They pumped her stomach to get rid of the pills. She's got some bad bruising on her chest and a broken rib from the CPR compressions."

"That's not so bad," I say.

Kerry looks at me wide-eyed. Clearly, he wasn't finished. "There's damage to her heart, Zander. To take that many diet pills with such a small body. And to live practically starved every day? She had a minor heart attack."

"But she'll be okay, right?" I sit forward in my seat.

Kerry shakes his head, like he can't answer the question for sure. "I hope so," he says. "I hope to God she'll be okay."

Madison calls the camp to let them know what's happened, and Kerry talks to more doctors who say Cassie has to stay in the hospital for at least three days of physical and psychiatric observation. I wait in my seat until they tell me I can go in and see her.

Eventually, Kerry comes to get me. I stand up, like my feet are spring loaded.

"She's sedated," he says. "But you can go in and see her."

It's a different world behind the doors. People walk around in scrubs with charts. Nurses laugh as they chat over coffee. So many doors open to rooms with so many people lying in beds hooked to machines. I stare down the giggling nurses. Nothing feels funny back here.

"It doesn't feel real, does it?" he asks.

I shake my head and look at Kerry. He sounds like he's talking from experience. His eyes search mine and, for a moment, I see what I can't believe I've never seen before—first Madison and now Kerry. He is broken, too.

When we both seem to acknowledge the moment, he says, "My brother, Charlie, was a total attention hog. He would do anything to make you notice him. I think that's why he loved being on stage. He was the best actor in our high school." Kerry rubs the back of his neck. "Later, I realized what he really loved was escaping reality."

"Was?" I ask, noting his use of past tense.

"Charlie hung himself my sophomore year of college. He was seventeen."

"Oh my God."

Kerry leans back against the white hospital wall and glances down at me. "Charlie was complicated and he drove me crazy sometimes." Kerry shakes his head. "Everything changed for me when Charlie died, and I knew what I was meant to do. I was already majoring in psychology. It just fit. I needed to save teenagers like him from making the biggest mistake of their lives."

"So you founded the camp." I sit back against the wall next to Kerry.

"If I could reverse time, I would tell Charlie that he's not alone. I would tell him that even though he felt lost, if he just waited and didn't give up, he would have found himself." Kerry looks down at his open palms. "But he left me. And I never got the chance to say it." He shrugs and smiles. "He would have loved Camp Padua."

Kerry seems to shake off the moment between us. He stands up straight, becoming the leader I've seen him as all summer. He points to a room number. "Cassie's in two seventy-one. You've got five minutes."

I nod. I'd take one second if that was all he offered.

He places a hand on my shoulder before I walk through the door. "You're a good friend, Zander. You saved her life."

I choke on the lump in my throat.

"You're a good brother, too. I guess we all have our crazy."

Kerry gives me a half-hearted smile. "Thank you."

I walk into Cassie's hospital room. The electric machines hum, one counting Cassie's heartbeat to an even rhythm. Another measures her oxygen intake. Even the computer hums.

I used to love these sounds. It meant life was still in my house. That Molly was still with me. I hate them now as I walk closer to Cassie. Today, they mean death.

I pull one of the doctors' spinning chairs over to the side of her bed, next to her cuffed-down arms. I touch them. Cuffs won't prevent her from hurting herself. They only prevent that for now.

I touch Cassie's warm skin and wrap my entire hand around hers, feeling her pulse. It beats under my thumb.

She's alive.

I bend my head down to the bed, like I'm bowing my head to pray. Like she's my own personal saint and I need her for help. Only her.

"Please forgive me," I say to Cassie. "Because *I* need you. I thought it was the other way around, but I was wrong. *I* need you." I say it over and over again until Kerry knocks on the door and tells me my time is up. "And Grover needs you, too. And Bek. We all need you."

"Time's up." Kerry leads me out of the room. He takes me back to the other side of the hospital. "And now, I think you need to head back to camp."

I pull back from his grip. "I'm not going. Not without her." Kerry looks tired, shadows circling under his eyes. "If it was your brother, would you have left him?" I ask. It's low, I know, but it's all I've got.

"Fine," he says, throwing his hands up. He walks away and down the hall. I return to the seat that I've been parked in for hours. Cassie's sweatshirt hangs over the back. I swing my legs over the side of the chair and rest. My eyelids start to pull downward, but I force them open. I nuzzle into the chair, covering myself in Cassie's sweatshirt, and imagine what Kerry looked like as a young person and what Charlie may have looked like. I start to cry for me and for Kerry. And before my cheeks can dry, I'm asleep.

I wake up to Kerry's voice. For a moment, I forget where I am, but as my eyes open and the white of the walls and the cups of coffee still sitting on the table come into view, it all comes rushing back.

I sit up quickly, my back sore from pressing into the wooden armrest while I slept. Kerry stands in the corner of the room, talking to a police officer.

"She has no family," the cop says, pointing down at the folder in his hands.

"Isn't there another option?" Kerry asks.

The cop shakes his head.

"What about her aunt?" I blurt out. They both look at me.

"Zander . . ." Kerry starts to say, but I cut him off.

"Cassie got a letter from her aunt. I heard her say it." My face feels tight from all the tears that have dried there, like my skin is dehydrated. I've lost all the water in my body.

Kerry dismisses the cop and comes to sit next to me. "Cassie doesn't have an aunt, Zander."

"But she said she got a letter from her Aunt Chey."

"Cassie got a letter from the foster woman she lives with named Cheyenne," Kerry says. "Her school in Detroit informed me about it just yesterday."

"Her school in Detroit?"

"Cassie comes to Camp Padua on a scholarship for kids who can't afford to come to camp but who would benefit from it. Her school contacted me about it a few years back in hopes it might help her."

"What?"

"Apparently, her foster parent, Cheyenne, can't handle Cassie anymore and she's sending her back," Kerry says.

"Sending her back where?" I ask. My throat feels like it might close. Tears break from my eyes even though I didn't think there was any water left in me. The world I thought spun in even circles is tilting on me. "Where are they sending her, Kerry?"

"To a group home for girls."

"No!" I yell, gathering the attention of the police officer. "She'll die there!"

Kerry looks around the hall and quiets me. "Zander, Cassie's been in ten different homes over the past ten years. Not one has been able to keep her."

"So people just give up on her? They just put her back into a broken system for broken people?"

"It's her best option."

"That's not an option." I point at Kerry. "That will kill her."

"There's nothing we can do."

"But you said we could all be found. You said that." I wipe tears from my cheeks. "I've been praying to Saint Anthony all summer. And now you're taking it back? That's what you're doing to her. Cassie will be lost forever. You said you wanted to save kids like Charlie, but you're killing her!"

I don't wait for Kerry to defend himself. I run down the hallway toward the exit sign, unable to be in this hospital a moment longer. I can't be in these concrete white walls with machines that keep people alive. This isn't living.

I burst through the hospital doors and into a parking lot. Cars buzz by on the street. Everything around me is concrete. I don't want concrete. I want camp. I want mosquitoes and trees and the sound of the water lapping on the beach of Lake Kimball. I want to hear Cassie make fun of Hannah. I want Bek to lie to me. I want Grover to kiss me and make this all go away. I want reality to just go the hell away.

I squeeze my arms around my chest as tight as I can. My breath comes in ragged pulls from the top of my lungs. The air is thick with smog and dirt and burned-out everyday life.

I scan the space around the hospital and find a tree. One lone green, leafy, alive tree in a sea of gray. I run toward it like it's my only way to survive.

When I'm in its shade, I fall down to my knees. The tree's full branches block the sun, and I curl up in the dirt. I pick a leaf off the ground and press it to my nose. It doesn't smell like the leaves do at Camp Padua. I ball it up in my fist and it crunches and breaks too easily.

Nothing that lives stays whole.

Everything eventually breaks.

After a while, I force myself up off the ground. Even in the shade, the sun hurts my eyes. I walk around the block, my feet dragging along the cement. I feel helpless and I hate it.

But when I see a drugstore across the street from the hospital, my spirits pick up. I can't go back into the hospital, not yet, but I can do something else.

I grab a basket and cruise the aisles of the drug store, quickly filling it with everything I need. When I get up to the clerk, he looks at me,, concerned.

"You okay, miss?"

"No. I'm never okay."

He shrugs, rings up my stuff, and asks for $15.74. I forgot things cost money out here, so I do the only thing I can think of. I tell him what happened. Every gory detail. My and Cassie's mistakes. I tell him and the line of customers behind me. They all listen intently. When I get to the end, the clerk looks at me, shocked.

"I'm glad your friend is okay," he says.

"Oh. She'll never be okay. Her heart is broken now." I shrug. "But she wasn't okay to begin with so . . ."

The woman behind me in line hands the clerk a twenty-dollar bill and says, "Broken hearts can heal. I'm a doctor. I've seen it."

"Thank you." I smile at her and look at all the people forming a line behind me. "You know what? This has been the best group share-apy session I've ever had."

CHAPTER 31

Dear Gerber Memorial Hospital,

Your beds are hard. Your sheets are starchy. And if one more person asks me to eat Jell-O, I'm going to file a lawsuit.

Kisses,
Cassie

When I round the corner on the hospital floor, Kerry lets out an exasperated sigh. "Where the hell were you?"

"I had to run an errand." I hold up my goods.

"Jesus, Zander."

"It's just Zander, but thank you for the compliment. You know, you really shouldn't take the Lord's name in vain."

He cocks his head, seemingly not amused, and picks up the sweatshirt lying on my chair. "You left this."

I take it from him. "I need to see her again."

"You have to do something for me first."

"Fine."

"Set everything down."

I follow his orders and place the bag and sweatshirt on a chair.

"Stand on one foot," Kerry says. "Put your arms out at your side for balance."

I look at him like he's losing it, but at this point we all are a little crazy, so I follow his instructions, wobbling a little bit at first, but then I settle into a steady place.

"Whatever you do, do not put your foot down until I tell you to. If you do, you can't see Cassie. If your foot touches the ground, you go back to camp."

I must look like a flamingo hovering on one leg in the middle of a hospital waiting room, but I keep my back straight and breathe.

Kerry smiles at me. "I'll be back." He starts to walk away.

"When?" I holler at him.

"Don't put your foot down." He leaves me and disappears down the hall.

I take a breath and stare at the wall. After a while my lifted leg starts to ache. Then my standing leg. Then my arms. Then I start to sweat. I make my breathing even and stare harder, but eventually my whole body hurts. Gravity pushes on me like a torture device, and I shake under the pressure. But I remind myself of Cassie in her hospital bed and how I need to see her. I *need* to.

It feels like forever until Kerry gets back. I've gone numb and I'm on the brink of tears. His face curls up into a broad smile as he sips a fresh coffee. I grit my teeth and look back at the wall.

"You can put your foot down."

The second my toes touch the ground, I collapse.

Kerry sits down in a chair and pats the seat next to him. I crawl over to him on my hands and knees.

"Perseverance is one of the final things we talk about at camp. It's an important life skill."

"Okay." I shake out my legs.

He squares his shoulders to me. "Charlie didn't think he had it in him. And he cut his life short before he could find out that he *did*." Kerry points to my legs. "Even when it hurts. Even when it feels like we can't go on. You need to make sure Cassie knows that. It might hurt like hell for her, but she can do it. And she'll listen to you."

Kerry goes back to the nurses' station then, and a few minutes later I get led back to Cassie's room. Finally.

I settle into the doctor's chair once again, setting the bag and sweatshirt on her bed. The nurse closes the door so that only a crack is left open. I sigh, relieved to be alone with my friend.

Her eyes are still closed and the machines are beeping, but I block it out. I take out the bottle of nail polish remover from the drugstore bag and a few cotton balls. I pick up Cassie's hand and inspect it. Just as I suspected, little bits of cracked, broken polish speckle her nails.

I take each finger and gently rub it down with a soaked cotton ball until all of the polish is gone. The slate is wiped clean.

I move to the other side of the bed and do her other hand. The nail polish remover smell covers up the death smell that seeps in through the crack in the door. I take the purple polish that I've chosen for Cassie out of the bag and, slowly, I paint her nails. I make sure to stay inside the lines. When I slip, I wipe it clean and start again.

I blow on them when I'm done, pulling in my breath and giving it back to her. Then I drape my sweatshirt over Cassie's small body and sit back in the seat next to her.

No one comes to get me, so I just sit. I rest my head down on the bed and just breathe with the ticking machines in the room.

At one point, I fall asleep. It's brief, and I wake up startled when Cassie's bed moves.

"Why does it smell like an Asian beauty salon in here?" she says, her voice raspy.

I stand up and move closer to make sure I'm not imagining her talking.

"Say something else," I say.

"Bek said I was going to hell, but this looks like a hospital." I laugh and launch myself on top of her. Cassie winces from pain.

"Sorry." I pull back. Reality seems to hit Cassie slowly. She pulls up on the restraints holding down her hands.

"What happened?" Cassie's face has turned sullen.

"I'll let the doctors tell you." I touch her arm.

"You brought my sweatshirt," she says. I smile when she takes back ownership of it and nod. "And you painted my nails?"

"You needed a fresh coat."

Cassie looks down at her hands. "I already messed one up."

I shrug as the doctors come into the room. "It was bound to happen. Nothing stays perfect forever. And I like it better that way."

"You're not going to leave me, Z, are you?"

I shake my head. "No, Cassie. I won't leave you. But you have to *promise* you won't leave me either."

Cassie looks up at the popcorn ceiling and nods slowly.

I pull a box of Lemonheads out of the bag and place it in her hand. "Take one in case of emergency."

Cassie looks back at me. A tear rolls down her cheek. "Thanks, Z."

CHAPTER 32

Dear Budget Airline,

I am writing this letter to inform you of my disappointment. I have not flown in many years and I must say, I was appalled at my experience with your airline. The lack of respect and basic humanity exhibited by your staff was atrocious. When I say I need to be somewhere, I need to be somewhere. You may be willing to delay a plane, but life cannot be delayed. It cannot.

Please excuse my tone. If you have children, you will understand.

Sincerely,
Nina Osborne

That night, I sleep in the chair and then move to the floor. A TV plays CNN news coverage over my head all night. Kerry stops trying to insist I go back to camp. Instead, he brings me a blanket from one of the nurses. He stays, too, sleeping in a chair with his arms folded over his chest and legs extended out.

In the morning, it takes a minute for me to remember where I am. Then I think I'm seeing a mirage—a long, beautiful, gangly mirage with a fat, squat, round one standing next to him.

I sit up straight as Grover walks over and kneels down next to me.

"I love watching you wake up."

I throw my arms around him and knock him over. Grover doesn't pull back because we're in public; he holds me tighter. He holds me the tightest he ever has.

"I'm sorry," he whispers in my ear. "I'm so sorry I wasn't watching her."

I ignore his words and press myself to him. I put my nose into his chest and breathe in. Grover smells like camp.

"I knew it," Kerry groans as he wakes up in his chair. When Grover puts up his finger to say something, Kerry stops him. "Save it. It's early and you're off camp property."

"Well, in that case . . ." Grover leans in and kisses me. The kiss is quick and light, but enough to wake me up more than the three cups of coffee I had yesterday.

Bek plops down in one of the waiting room seats. *"Mon amour. Comment va-t-elle?"*

"She's okay," I tell him. "Well, not okay, but okay for now."

"Bek got Madison to bring us here," Grover whispers to me. "He went on a hunger strike."

"Bek refused food?"

Grover nods. "He said he was lovesick, which according to Bek causes pain, nausea, occasional vomiting, and a lawsuit brought on by his dad, who's the mayor of Toronto. And then he demanded we get taken to the hospital to find a cure. Madison conceded and said it must have taken a lot of perseverance for a kid like Bek to refuse food."

I glance at Bek, who's staring at the ceiling, his foot tapping on the ground.

It takes a few hours before they'll let us go back and see her. When we finally get to her room, Cassie is staring out the window.

The restraints are gone today. I'm thankful Grover and Bek didn't see them. Bek sits on the end of the bed as Cassie looks at us with a shocked face. She clearly wasn't expecting all of us. Bek touches her feet, which are covered up by a few layers of blankets. Even covered, Cassie looks cold.

"Well, Sticks, that was quite a performance. Not quite what I expected, but you've always kept me on my toes, which is what I love about you," Grover says. He emphasizes the end part. The love part.

Bek hiccups as he sits crying at the end of the bed. He bends down and kisses Cassie's feet over and over.

"*Mon amour. Mon amour. Mon amour,*" he repeats.

Cassie's face paints in horror, but she doesn't move. Grover touches her hand. "You can't lie about love," he says. He inspects her nails. "Nice color, by the way. Totally you."

I smile at her, and in the most beautiful way possible, Cassie smiles back.

At the end of our time, I ask the boys to give me a minute.

"I'll see you soon, Sticks," Grover says to Cassie. "Now you say it back."

"I'll see you soon, Cleve."

"That's a promise," he says.

"That's a promise," Cassie says. He exhales a large breath, and he and Bek leave the room.

I pull up my seat next to her bed. I'll gladly give it back to the doctor if he can promise Cassie never has to come here again.

"Why did you lie to me about your aunt?"

Cassie looks off at the window. "Because it isn't your problem."

"Like hell it isn't my problem." My voice rises.

Her eyes come back to me. "What are you going to do, Z? Erase my past? Change it? The past may be gone, but it's firmly in place. You can't do anything about it."

"I could have at least listened."

"Listening does nothing."

"Stop acting like you're alone," I yell and stand up, the tears starting again. "You're not alone. You made me need you! You made me love you! And now I need you to tell me you won't give up again. Even if it hurts like hell. You can't give up. I won't let you take that away from me."

Cassie looks at me wide-eyed as I plop back down in the seat.

"God, Z, you're selfish." And then she places her hand on top of mine. "You need me?" I nod over and over, tears falling on my shirt. "I've never been needed before."

"Well, get used to it," I say.

"Hey, Z?"

"What?"

"Clearly you're not over your lesbian phase. I hope Cleve knows."

I nod, wiping a tear from my cheek, and smile. "He's kind of excited about it."

Cassie laughs again and the room brightens.

Before I walk out, I turn back to Cassie and repeat the words she said to Dori just a few weeks ago. "I can't believe you tried to kill yourself with pills. What a sissy fucking suicide."

Cassie smiles. "Thanks, Z."

The waiting room smells different when I get there. I breathe in again. Rose perfume. My eyes scatter through the people around me. Grover and Bek sit watching the TV.

And then I find the source of the smell. I gasp and yell at the same time. It's my mom.

HOPE

CHAPTER 33

Dear Detroit Child Services,

We reject your ruling.

Sincerely,

Cassandra Dakota LaSalle's best friend,

Zander . . . and her mother

My mom looks up from where she's standing at the nurses' station. Her eyes light up the second she sees me, and mine must be doing the same.

I run to hug her and smash myself so hard into her skinny body that she almost falls over.

"Mom. I'm so glad you're here." I press my face into her neck. Her skin feels like sunlight. Like she brought the dry Arizona wind with her.

My mom grabs my face with both of her hands and lifts it up. She inspects me and wipes a finger across my cheek.

"You're crying," she says in a wobbly voice.

I nod as more tears fall. "Sorry I waited this long."

She grabs me, rocking me back and forth. "It's okay, baby. I'm sorry, too."

We continue hugging, standing in the waiting room. I guess happiness can be found in a hospital if you stay long enough.

"I'm so glad to see you," she whispers in my ear.

"Me, too." And I mean it.

Someone taps my shoulder and I look up.

"I thought I should introduce myself to my future mother-in-law." Grover rocks back on his heels. My mom inspects my smiling face again with a pensive look on her own. Like she can't believe what she's seeing.

From head to toe, she takes in the long boy next to me. "This must be Grover."

"At your service, Zander's mom."

"It's nice to meet you, Grover. You have quite an interesting name."

He winks at my mom. "You have no idea." And then he takes out his notebook. I guess we all have a few habits that are hard to break. "I'm gonna need to ask you a few questions."

Madison takes Grover and Bek back to camp. Even Kerry leaves for a few hours to shower and sleep. But I stay with my mom. We sit in the waiting room, me in a chair that permanently dips in the center because I've sat in it for so long.

"I still can't believe you're here," I say.

My mom pulls a granola bar out of her purse. It's not her brand. She inspects the wrapper and shrugs. "It was all they had in the airport." She snaps the bar in half and gives me one of the pieces. She takes a bite. And I smile. "The camp called when everything happened. They said you insisted on going with the girl. That you pulled your friend out of the water." My mom takes another bite of the granola bar and chews slowly. "I couldn't just sit in Arizona anymore. I needed to see you."

I tell her everything. I start at the beginning, the exact moment Cassie walked in the cabin door.

"She said what?" Her face looks appalled.

I go on from there, not leaving out a single detail until it comes to Grover. I leave that out. That is meant for me, him, a broom closet, and my memory.

I tell her about the night it all came crashing down. I tell her how scared and sad and broken I felt. My mom looks in my eyes as I cry again. She brushes the hair out of my face and nods.

"They're going to send her to a group home. And she'll be alone, again. But Cassie can't be alone, Mom." My sobs come at an uncontrollable pace. "She can't."

"It's okay, baby." She hugs me.

"No, it's not okay," I whisper in her ear.

When my mom says she needs to make a few phone calls, particularly to my dad, I sneak through the automatic doors and down the hallway to Cassie's room.

She's asleep in her bed, though the machines still beep around her. I watch her legs, waiting for one of them to move. She has more life left in her. I know it.

Cassie rolls onto her side and exhales a deep breath. I do the same.

Slowly, one of her eyes opens just the littlest bit, her hand lifts, and her middle finger pops up. Yes. She has more life left in her.

CHAPTER 34

Dear Molly,

Life is strange. I don't know why things happen the way they do. But I do know that living is just that. It's a verb. An action.

In French, vivre.

To live.

I was brought back to life this summer.

I was found.

And it feels *good.*

Love,

Zander

Cassie comes back to camp on the last day. Kerry pulls up in front of the gates and looks into the backseat. I grab Cassie's hand. Her eyes are tired and her body looks like one harsh wind might break it, but she's stronger than that. Broken heart and all.

Kerry nods at Cassie and she does the same back. We drive through the boundary that marks the line between reality and camp.

I help Cassie out of the car. Campers scatter around, hugging parents and lugging bags. A few stare at us, but Cassie keeps her eyes on the ground.

I walk her to the cabin, my arm under hers for support, like she did for me weeks ago.

When we walk through the door, everyone in the entire cabin sits on their beds waiting. Cassie looks into all of their eyes. I see a flash of fear. And then each one comes up to her and offers her their gimp key chain.

"To remind you of who you are," Katie says.

"And that life takes teamwork." Hannah places hers in her hand.

Dori comes up next. "And that trust isn't such a bad word after all."

I take mine out of my pocket. "That you *are* courageous."

Madison steps forward. She lays the statue of St. Anthony of Padua in the palm of Cassie's hand.

"To remind you that life takes perseverance through the hard times, but there is always a way to be found."

Cassie clasps them all tightly in her grip and stares down at her hand.

"Thanks for saving my life, Madison."

"Actually." Madison nudges Cassie in the shoulder. "I prefer it when you call me Mads."

The whole cabin starts to laugh. A moment later the bathroom door opens. My mom walks out, holding up one of Cassie's cropped tank tops.

"Oh, this is completely unacceptable." She tosses it in the garbage can.

"Excuse me." Cassie looks at me with shock and a dash of anger painted on her face. "That's my stuff you're throwing out. Who is this woman?"

I shrug as Cassie crosses the room, angry that my mom is rummaging around in her drawer.

"I'm just making sure there are no more pills."

"What the hell is going on?"

My mom stops and looks at her. "First rule, you eat what I cook. Second rule, you wear what I tell you to wear. Third rule, the only pills you'll be taking are ones prescribed to you by real doctors. And you will be seeing doctors."

"You're Zander's mom, aren't you?" Cassie says.

"Now, Cassie, if you're willing to live by my rules, we have an extra room at our house." My mom smiles at me from across the room. "It's about time someone actually lived in it."

A gasp breaks from Cassie's lips, but she still doesn't move.

"What about the group home?"

"We still have to figure that one out," my mom says. "It's gonna be a bit of a fight. Are you ready to fight, Cassie?" She nods, her eyes on my mom like she's a ghost or maybe even a saint. My mom pats Cassie on the back. "Good, because I don't let go of things easily. I'll fight until the very last second if I have to."

I walk up and whisper in Cassie's ear. "All that hoping had to be good for something, right?"

She looks at me and then my mom. "I don't believe in that word," Cassie says.

"Well . . ." My mom hooks her arm over Cassie's shoulder. "It's a good time to start."

Later, when I'm packing, I unzip my bag and find the window screw Cassie gave me the first night of camp. I go into the bathroom and jam the screw back into place. It's no fun when you can escape easily.

We stand on the deck overlooking Lake Kimball. The water glistens in the fading sunlight. A slight breeze blows my hair away from my face.

"I'm sorry you never got green," I say to Cassie.

She squints as she looks out at the water. "I got something else instead."

"Amen." Grover smiles.

A voice bellows up behind us, and we all turn to see Bek running across the deck with a short blond man trailing behind him.

"I wanted you guys to meet my dad," he says, out of breath.

"This is your dad?" Cassie says to the man.

"Mr. Trebek," he replies and holds out his round hand.

We all laugh. Even Cassie.

And as the sun fades into the night, Grover leans over and kisses me.

"Only one in fifty long-distance relationships last."

"I've always hated odds," I say.

"Oddly enough, me, too," he says.

"I'm glad you finally have the courage to acknowledge that." I smile at Grover. "So will you write me?"

"Where should I send my letters?"

I take Grover's notebook from his back pocket and turn to the page I wrote on weeks ago. There, in my handwriting, is my address. I point to it.

"You've had me all along."

He clutches the notebook to his chest. "I love reality."

"We have one last thing to do." Cassie pulls the fork she stole that first day from her back pocket. We all eye her as she walks over to the wooden railing that lines the deck of the mess hall. Using the fork, she etches a word into the wood. Then she hands it down the line and we all add our initials, until our names are permanently left at Camp Padua.

The four of us turn from Lake Kimball and start the long walk to our cars.

"So next year? Same time? Same place?" Grover asks.

"I wouldn't miss it," Bek says.

"Me neither." I smile up at Grover as he reaches his arm around my waist.

"What about you, Sticks? See you next year?"

She glances over her shoulder and takes one last look at the word she's carved into the wood—*hope*.

"Absolutely." Then she grabs Bek's hand. "This doesn't mean I like you."

"Of course not." Bek smiles a true grin. "You love me."

I reach my arm around Cassie and pull her in close. "Let's go home."

As we walk away, I steal a glance back over my shoulder and see Grover lift his arm high in the air and fist pump the sky.

ACKNOWLEDGMENTS

First—a huge, love-filled thank-you to Jessica Park. You always manage to help me find my way when I'm lost. You took a chance on a phone call with a random stranger a few years ago, and look at us now—soul mates. This book is what it is because of you. Thank you.

To my agent and friend, Renee Nyen—you loved this book from the beginning. We have seen some crazy days, but we made it through together. I am so grateful for everything you do. Thank you.

To my editor, Jason Kirk—I could not have asked for a better person to take this book and make it soar. Your enthusiasm is infectious. (And a special shout-out to Coco Williams!)

To all the beta readers, friends and family, and fans who have championed my writing and my books, who have invited me into their homes for book clubs, who have asked me to speak at their schools, who have sat in my living room and brainstormed idea after idea—thank you! Thank you! Thank you!

And to Anna, who said, "Why don't you name him Grover Cleveland?"

The rest is . . . history.

ABOUT THE AUTHOR

Photo © 2014 Cara Vescio

Rebekah Crane is the author of three young-adult novels—*Playing Nice*, *Aspen*, and *The Odds of Loving Grover Cleveland*. She found a passion for young-adult literature while studying secondary English education at Ohio University. After having two kids and living and teaching in six different cities, Rebekah finally settled in the foothills of the Rocky Mountains to write novels and work on screenplays. She now spends her day carpooling kids or tucked behind a laptop at 7,500 feet, where the altitude only enhances the writing experience.